SF VOICES

ALFRED BESTER
ROBERT SILVERBERG
BRIAN ALDISS
JAMES GUNN
GARDNER DOZOIS
NORMAN SPINRAD
GORDON DICKSON
BEN BOVA
TED WHITE
JACK WILLIAMSON
L. SPRAGUE DE CAMP
FRANK BELKNAP LONG
GAHAN WILSON
JERRY POURNELLE

interviewed by
Darrell
Schweitzer

Typeset by Nickelodeon Graphic Arts Service
1131 White, Kansas City, MO 64126

Contents

Dedication:

This book is gratefully dedicated to those authors who donated their time to make the project possible, and to Francis J. Flutter who lent me a demented tape recorder.

3

acknowledgements:

The interview with Alfred Bester was originally published in *Amazing,* May 1976, copyright © 1976 by Ultimate Publishing Company.

The interview with Robert Silverberg was originally published in *Amazing,* January 1976, copyright © 1975 by Ultimate Publishing Company.

The interview with Brian Aldiss is published here for the first time.

The interview with James Gunn was originally published in *The Drummer* for October 22, 1974, copyright © 1974 by Tixeon Inc.

The interview with Gardner Dozois was originally published in *The Drummer* for June 11, 1974, copyright © 1974 by Tixeon Inc.

The interview with Norman Spinrad appears here for the first time.

The interview with Gordon Dickson appears here for the first time.

The interview with Ted White appears here for the first time.

The interview with Ben Bova appears here for the first time.

The interview with Gahan Wilson appears here for the first time.

The interview with L. Sprague de Camp was originally published in *The Drummer* for August 13, 1974, copyright © 1974 by Tixeon Inc. It was reprinted in *Science Fiction Review 15,* and a small amount of original material added by the editor, Richard E. Geis, is included here with Mr. Geis' gracious permission. Copyright © 1975 by Richard E. Geis.

The interview with Frank Belknap Long originally appeared in *Nyctalops 11,* copyright © 1975 by Harry O. Morris, Jr.

The interview with Jack Williamson was originally published in *Star-Wind,* Vol. 1, No. 2. copyright © 1976 by the Starwind Press.

The interview with Jerry Pournelle appears here for the first time.

Introduction

The purpose of this book is to allow you, the science fiction reader, to know your authors better, to go beyond the dustjacket squib and show what sort of person an individual writer is, what his interests are, where he came from. A successful interview helps to put a voice and a personality behind a byline. After conducting these interviews I hear the writer talking every time I read one of his stories. His art has become a little more individualised, which is what any worthwhile art should be.

A slightly less lofty but equally important purpose for the existence of this collection is that it promotes the work of the authors included herein. Have you read something by everyone on the contents page? If not you're missing a great deal. Correct this oversight at once. It's not polite to try and get acquainted with somebody whose work you don't know.

This volume is the first of a series. *SF Voices No. 2* will contain interviews with Fritz Leiber, Poul Anderson, Lin Carter, Hal Clement, Robert Bloch, Lester del Rey, Frederik Pohl, Fred Saberhagen, and several others. A few of these interviews will appear in *Amazing*, no doubt, but certainly not all of them. Some may appear in more obscure journals, and certainly there will be some originals, so it'll be worth your while to get the book. It's also worth your while to read something by every one of those authors too.

—Darrell Schweitzer
Strafford, Pa.
November 13, 1975

Alfred Bester

Q. You state here [in the essay, "SF & the Renaissance Man" by Alfred Bester in *The Science Fiction Novel*, edited by B. Davenport (Advent)] that the purpose of art is to entertain and/or move its audience, and that science fiction can entertain but not move. Why is that?

Bester: Because most SF writers don't know enough about people to write real people with real problems, and you can't move a reader unless you write about real people with real problems. Alas, I'm sorry to knock my colleagues in the profession, but most SF writers know very little about life and very little about people, and therefore the reader finds it difficult to be moved by them. This is why SF calls to itself people who are mostly science oriented rather than drama oriented. If there were more drama, more reality of human nature in SF it would be drawing an even wider audience that it does now. As it is it mostly draws the people who are just curious about science.

Q. Is this a limitation of the form or the people who write it?

Bester: No, no, it's a limitation of the writers themselves. What I say about science fiction is also true of television, women's magazines, skin magazines, everything. The difficulty we have in the United States is that most writers—not all, but most writers—have not yet grown up. We're not adults, and that is the difficulty we have. I think for every American novel you read that you enjoy, that's real, there are at least fifty that you read a chapter or two of and then throw it down and say, "Whoever this is doesn't know what the hell he or she is talking about. These people aren't real. I'm not interested." Now this goes for SF and it goes for all forms of writing. Since we're discussing SF I'll limit it to SF, but I really don't limit it in my mind to any particular form or medium.

6

Q. Why do you think there are so many overgrown adolescents writing sf?

Bester: Because this country is an adolescent country; our culture is an adolescent culture. Here's an example. In *TV Guide* a couple of leading TV scriptwriters were beefing like crazy that TV didn't permit them to do "serious writing," which is preposterous. I know all the guys. I know what they're doing now—they're doing the same thing that we all did thirty years ago—but your average American writer gets so *serious* about writing. It means to the average American, who is rather adolescent, something which is serious must be profound, meaningful, heavy, weighty, and this is a result of a lack of maturity. There's no such thing as a sophisticated child, and yet we seem to be sophisticated children. Ken Tynan put it best when he spoke of Americans as being sophisticated illiterates. That's what we are, as writers and as readers.

Q. Why are we sophisticated illiterates?

Bester: We're sophisticated because of the media. We're very hip about everything that's going on. Why are we illiterates? Because I don't think many of us received a decent education, and I don't think that if they have received a decent education it has stuck with them, point one. Point two, I don't think the average American has had much experience in life, genuine experience. We have been very sheltered. It's only in the past generation or so that the young people have—*thank God*—been pointing out to the adults "You don't know what it's all about." I have believed for a long time—it's very cynical—that this country is not going to grow up until we lose a war, until we get licked and then occupied. Then we'll grow up, but not until then. So far we've been—well they tell that old gag about the couple guys from Boston who were on a train from New York to Boston and one of them says to the other, "Whatever happened to Jennifer?" "Oh she's living in New York." "Oh is she really? What's she doing?" "Oh I have very bad news about her. She's doing something awful." "What is she doing?" "She's a prostitute." "Oh thank God!" said the other one. "For a moment I thought you were going to say she's living on capital." We in the states have been living on capital all our lives, which is why ecology came along too late and says for God's sake, don't destroy this heritage of ours. We have been getting fat and rich destroying our heritage and now we're beginning to wake up just a little bit with the oil squeeze.

Q. Do you think it's possible to—?

Bester: To grow us up? No, as I said before, the only thing that's going to do it is for us to get licked in a war, nothing else, because we're fat and lazy and don't know what the score is. If I were president of the US I would pass a law, the first law I would pass, which would require every American citizen to spend two years living abroad in Europe, China, anywhere, to learn what the score really is.

Q. Do we then find greater maturity in foreign writings?

Bester: Foreign writing? Yes, indeed, yes.

Q. Even foreign SF?

Bester: Oh I haven't read much foreign SF—I haven't had the opportunity to read much of it, but the little that I've read—is it more mature? In a sense, yes. I've read mostly the French writers, and they seem to have a delicious sense of humor which is of course a part of maturity.

[pause]

Hey—I was going to tell you the story about the elephant that robbed the jewelry store. 47th Street is the big jewelry center in New York and this jeweler comes to his shop—it's a very elegant shop, selling precious stones—he comes quite early one morning to get some bookkeeping done, and he arrives just in time to see a truck back up in front of his store and an elephant gets out of the back of the truck and with its trunk it smashes the window and scoops up all the goodies and gets back into the truck and the truck drives off. The guy is absolutely flabbergasted and he calls the cops at once, of course. The police come and they start asking questions. Well what kind of truck was it? It was a rental truck. Did you see the guy who drove it? No, no, I can't give you a description. Well was it an African elephant or an Indian elephant? What do you mean? There's a difference? Yeah, the African elephant has big ears which stick out wide on both sides of his head, and the Indian elephant has little small ears that stick close to its head. And the guy says, 'Ears, ears, ears! How could I tell? The elephant wore a stocking over its head.'

[laughter]

Q. With some pretense of seriousness, I notice in this essay here, you are talking about the limitations of science fiction as a form. What do you think they are?

Bester: The limitations of SF? That's a tough question. Let's see. [pause] I think the main limitation of SF is that it must, *ipso-facto* be make believe. You enjoy reading make believe stories now and then, but not as a steady diet. I think that's about its only limitation. That and the fact that too many of the writers are rather childish and don't write about human beings. You see, when I write I try very hard; with or without success I don't know; to use science as an excuse to present human beings with new problems, new conflicts, and they try and figure out how they're going to solve them, how they're going to cope with them. Sometimes they do cope; sometimes they fail. But for me science is only the excuse to hit people with novel problems. That's what I try to do. When I read SF I read it with the same thing in mind. I want to read about real people facing the problems of the future or of extrapolation. And I do read stories like that occasionally, but not as often as I would like to. Usually you find that the men who are best on extrapolation of science are weakest on characters. You find that the people who are best on character don't know enough science to write science fiction.

Q. Well then why did you turn to SF when you did? Back in 1939, when your first story appeared, the field was not exactly producing sublime classics of literature.

Bester: For a very simple reason. Of course as a boy I fell madly in love with science fiction. I read it constantly. I took a crack at writing because I didn't know what else to do. So what kind of writing to do? The kind of writing I knew best, which would be science fiction. I was not likely to attempt a Dostoyevskian novel or a Tolstoyan novel, or even a Dickensian novel. I knew that I had no capacity for that. SF was a small enough, limited enough field and I had studied science. I had taken my degree as a matter of fact in the scientific disciplines here at the University of Pennsylvania. So I knew enough science and I knew enough of the field to take a crack at it. And I was very lucky. I had a funny experience. I was chatting with Robert Heinlein the other day— oh, the other month it must have been—and I was interviewing him for *Publisher's Weekly*, and I said, 'Robert, how did you write your first science fiction story?' And he said, *'Thrilling Wonder* was running a contest for the best story by an amateur and they were offering this fifty dollar prize, and so I wrote this story, but it ran 7000 words, and I had heard that a magazine called *Astounding* was paying a cent a word, so I submitted it to *Astounding* first, and they bought it.' And I said to him, 'Robert you son of a bitch, I won that contest and you beat me by $20.' And of course winning the contest was purely a fluke. It was only with the help of the editors who showed me how to rewrite the story and make it tolerable—that's all it was, tolerable—and having sold one story I tried again, and again, and again. And very slowly I began to write SF, but when the big Superman explosion started I shifted over to comic books. They needed writers very badly. And then from comics I switched to radio, from radio to television, and I kept moving on all the time. That's all.

Q. How did you get back into SF?

Bester: I kept going back all the time because, for example, in script writing very often the networks or the clients would not permit me to use an idea that I liked very much. They'd say, 'Well you know, it's too novel for the public. They won't understand it.' Or else, 'Oh no, it would be too expensive to do. The budget can't stand it.' Now some of these ideas I left in my gimmick book, my commonplace book, but others just bugged me so I had to write them, and since they were kind of off trail I wrote them as SF which gave me a completely free hand. And so that's how I would go to SF and go away from it and go back to it.

Q. Have you ever had opportunities to do SF in the media?

Bester: Oh yes, but I've always turned them down, because the producers of the shows wanted the kind of science fiction that was being written in the 1920s, and I didn't want any part of that. It was too far back for me. Yes, I've gone out to the Coast several times, and each time

I would talk to the producers and they'd still be looking for the comic book character—what's his name?

Q. Flash Gordon?

Bester: Yes, they're still looking for Flash Gordon. So I don't want any part of that. You have to move with the times.

Q. Well there have been serious attempts to do adult SF on television. They haven't been too successful.

Bester: No, they haven't been too successful, and I think I know why. I think they haven't been successful for the same reason that SF films haven't been very successful. Your TV audience and your film audience are relatively inexperienced, so the best you can give them is Flash Gordon. Anything beyond that, anything mature in SF terms, is just too much for them.

Q. Do you think it's possible, with this adolescent audience and even more adolescent industry—

Bester: Well, no, it's unfair as far as SF goes to call it an adolescent audience. Let's say that it's an inexperienced audience. In SF terms an unsophisticated audience, so you have to give them the simplistic kind of SF.

Q. Is it possible to get anything better?

Bester: Certainly, and soon as you educate your audience you give them better and better. Sure, but it'll take time.

Q. It is generally agreed that there is no work in SF right now which is to be considered among the greatest works of human literature. Do you think we'll ever get such a work?

Bester: Well, you know, it all depends on your definition of the greatest works of literature. That's a tough one, really. You take a novel, for example, like Reade's *The Cloister and The Hearth*. That's high style, almost picaresque writing—well it's high adventure writing. Theoretically this would be the equivalent of a science fiction novel. Have there been SF novels equivalent to that? What's my answer? No. Why not? Jesus Christ that's a rough question to answer. How about *Mary Poppins*, which is surely a classic? Certainly if it's not SF it is fantasy and delicious fantasy too. So there have been fantasies which have been classics. *The Wind In The Willows* for example. There's a great classic for you, a beast fable. *The Wind In The Willows* is marvellous. Have there been SF classics. How about *The War of the Worlds*? That's a magnificent novel, really magnificent. That's great literature. So SF can achieve it.

Q. Something that Robert Silverberg once brought up in an interview was that SF had yet to produce its Shakespeare.

Bester: Well so has literature. [laughs] After Shakespeare what? That s.o.b., he's the death of every writer. He's so great that you're always writing against him and losing. But we produced one Shakespeare, period, and so to ask for another is asking too much. Why not say has SF yet to produce its Dickens or its Reade or its Nancy Mitford? I don't know. How about Lewis Carroll? SF has yet to produce its Lewis Carroll. That I think is a fair comparison. These kinds of great talents only show up once every four or five generations. We have to be patient in between, that's all. Someone will come along in SF. For all we know some novel which we take for granted, we may discover if we live long enough, that in time it will become a great classic of literature. *The Space Merchants*, which I think is one of the finest SF novels ever written, may well turn out to be a classic.

Q. Do you think such a great novel will be recognized?

Bester: No, of course not.

Q. Later?

Bester: Later, surely. It'll be recognized later, and it'll be a great surprise to us to find out, "What? That thing's a classic? It was just another book I read, that's all."

Q. Do you see anybody in the field right now with classic potential?

Bester: Oh man, that's a tough one. You must understand, I am not knocking any writer—I absolutely refuse to do that—but the writers that I praise, that appeal to me the most, may not necessarily appeal to the world. For example, Theodore Sturgeon. I have always adored everything that Sturgeon has ever written. And if anyone is capable of producing an all time classic it certainly is Ted. Who else? Well you know I am a great, *great* admirer of Cyril Kornbluth's, and a great admirer of Henry Kuttner. Kuttner I thought was like God, and alas, alas, alas, Kuttner died, but some of his short stories are great classics. Do you remember one called "Vintage Season?" He wrote it under the name of O'Donnell. Gee, that's a great story. He had the master touch. Why am I still alive and why is he dead? It should be the other way around, because he really had it.

Q. In this essay you mention that the appeal of SF is basically that of "Arrest Fiction," meaning it's something that grabs ahold of someone—

Bester: Oh yes, sure. Again I'll quote Robert Heinlein. He said, 'Look what I do. I grab you off the street, grab you by the lapels—I never let go—and I shake you.' Well, that's arrest fiction. That's what he does. I do it in a different way. I shoot bullets past their heads. But it's the same damn thing. I mean you shake them up and knock 'em as silly as you can, hopefully entertaining them while you're doing it.

Q. How do you design a story to shake the reader?

11

Bester: Well first I have to shake myself. One example. Ben Bova [editor of *Analog*] had exactly the same reaction. In this novel that *Analog* is running now, there came a point at which it suddenly dawned on me that I would have to kill off my favorite character, a lady. And it just came on me, slowly but surely, Alfie you gotta kill her. The cast of characters and the balance of the story require it. It's absolutely necessary. Well I couldn't write for a week. I just couldn't bring myself to write the death scene, because I loved her so much and she was such a part of me. And finally I got up the guts, and I killed her. And then I went into complete shock and couldn't write for a week after that. She was dead. My baby was dead. And I was delighted when Ben got the manuscript and read it and said, 'Alfie when you killed off so and so I was in complete shock. It killed me that you killed her.' I said, 'Yeah, it hit me the same way.' I have to surprise myself and astonish myself and shake myself up. And if I can do it to myself, hopefully it will have the same effect on the reader.

Q. Do you consciously use stylistic tricks to achieve this, such as the unusual typography in *The Stars My Destination?*

Bester: No, that's not done for the purpose of shaking them up. It's done because of the attempt on my part to create an entire milieu, to build an entire civilization. And I find that I must in order to do that use visual as well as literary imagery. It's not done just for the sake of a trick. It's done because it will add some color to the particular milieu in which the story is taking place. That's all.

Q. Did you have a lot of trouble with the typesetters and proofreaders on that and on *The Demolished Man?*

Bester: No, not really. No trouble at all. My editors understood what was being done and monitored the production of the books very carefully. Where I've had the most difficulty and still do is where I deliberately use bad grammar. You'll always find a copy checker who's going to clean up your grammar. You know, they did that to Ring Lardner once. It's a classic story about copy checkers. Ring Lardner of course was famous for writing stories from the standpoint of a narrator who as often as not was a dumb ballplayer or dumb prizefighter or something, who used miserable grammar, and one publishing house published one of his stories and they cleaned up all the grammar, which of course destroyed the story. They had missed the entire point. Now the same thing happened to me when I quoted a line of Ring Lardner's, "Writeing is a nag." Of course 'writing' is misspelled, and what the character was trying to say was "writing is a knack" and that's the way Lardner wrote it. And that's what I used for a piece I wrote for an English publication and dammit if the copy checkers didn't clean it up, and I had to send the copy back and say "Stet! Stet! Stet! Sic! Sic! Sic!" This is the way it is. I have this trouble all the time. As a matter of fact Dianna King at *Analog* had a hell of a problem because sometimes my misspellings were deliberate and other times they were accidents. And she had to figure out whether it was deliberate or stupidity.

Q. Well I just ran out of questions.

Bester: Oh that's all right, I'll ask a few questions. What aspect of SF do you think readers are most interested in about writers, the authors of SF?

Q. About the authors? What kind of person writes this. I think the guy who doesn't read SF often will ask where they get those crazy ideas, and the fan is probably a frustrated would-be writer himself, and he'll say, "How do they do it?" And the fan who is not a would-be writer—there are a few occasionally—might wonder what kind of person this is who is producing this.

Bester: Well in the sense of does he have a trick or secret that I can learn so I can write it too?

Q. I don't think it works that way.

Bester: I know it doesn't work that way, but do you think that they think it works that way?

Q. Oh yes, especially if you talk to non-writers, the ones who have a very exaggerated concept of the value of a story idea. You know, 'I've got this great idea for a story—'

Bester: I don't have the time, so all you have to do is write it for me.

Q. Yeah, the ones who don't realize that stories are people and images and experiences. They think it's just the idea.

Bester: And as a matter of fact I've already said, and it's perfectly true, that you can take the identical idea and give it to six different writers and each will produce an entirely different story because after all the art is the man and the man is the art and you write what you are, you paint what you are, you sculpt what you are, you compose what you are. It's unavoidable. And one of the difficulties I had with young writers was trying to explain to them as gently as possible, 'Look, write only what you know.' You haven't had much experience yet, you're only 21, so don't write about things you don't know about. Just write your experiences. You will eventually, as time passes, grow, experience more, and your horizons as a writer will enlarge. But be content with your limited horizons now and try, off duty as it were, to enlarge your experiences. Go out and have experiences. I used to tell that to Jim Blish all the time. I remember in reviewing one of Jim Blish's books, 'For God's sake, Jim, will you go out and chase ladies, gamble, rob a bank, do something. Get experience, because although your science is great your characters are completely unreal.'

Q. How important do you think everyday experiences are in writing SF? Won't they give the story a flavor which will badly date it?

Bester: No. I'm going to use you. Someday I'll use you. I don't know what I'll do with you but I'll use you. I'm a packrat. My wife calls me a cesspool. Nothing goes to waste. I'll use you. I used to know a guy, an Englishman, who was a colleague of mine and we were writing the same TV show together. He was doing the research on it and I was writing the script. He also wrote himself, but he didn't really believe he was creating unless he made it up out of whole cloth. He had to invent everything. And I would say, 'For Christ's sake, this character is not real. Will you use somebody you know if you need a character?' No, he had to invent everything. As a result his stories were completely unbelievable.

Q. How do you account for an imaginary world fantasy, such as *The Lord of the Rings* or the James Branch Cabell books?

Bester: I hate it. Sure, I hate Cabell. When I was a kid I used to enjoy reading it only because of the little sex passages in it, and you know when you're a kid you like to read sexy stuff, but I hate Cabell. As for the *Ring* cycle, that's unique. Only it had some sensational chapters in the first novel. He had some other chapters which were incredibly dull. But I just prefer to think of the great chapters.

Q. Well, is this because his invention flagged or maybe because Tolkien was a dull person?

Bester: I wish I knew. I don't know the guy. If I'd interviewed him I would have found out.

Q. What happens if a writer writes himself into a story and no one is interested?

Bester: He shouldn't write it. He should give up writing and go and be an honest man and work in Gimbels or something. If you lose it you lose it. There's nothing you can impose on the reader. The reader owes you nothing. You owe everything to the reader, to entertain him. If you've lost it, too bad.

Q. Basically a writer has to be an interesting person to begin with?

Bester: That I don't know. Some of the most brilliant writers I've met have been very dull people in real life. Their writing it so happens can be fantastic.

Q. Maybe this is because they put everything in their writing and there's nothing left.

Bester: It could be. I could easily be. I think that's the answer myself but I couldn't swear to it.
                              [pause]
Running out of gas or out of tape?

Q. Both. You exhausted the first line of questioning so quickly—

Bester: Well, let's think up some more questions. Why don't you ask me 'Do you think your stories should have illustrations?' I don't think my stories should have illustrations. I would prefer to think that I draw word pictures for the reader and it's a collaboration between me and the reader, and I can give him the inspiration for a picture and he'll draw his own picture, and I think the illustrations would only get in the way of that.

Q. You were talking earlier about the use of unusual typography to create visual rather than purely literary images. Couldn't a collaboration with the artist help further this?

Bester: Oh man, you're right, but it never works that way. Now I talk as an editor. I have never, never been able to communicate with art directors, with artists, with photographers. There are one or two exceptions, but as a rule it's been impossible. I think it's because I am very visual in my writing; I am *writing* visually. I'm not photographing; I'm writing visually. The art director types are purely visual and for them words are meaningless really, and so for me it has always been difficult to communicate with them because all I can use are words. I can sit down and make a sketch or something like that, but for them, professionals, that doesn't work at all. Yes, a collaboration would be wonderful, but you will find that ninety-nine times out of a hundred the art director, the artist, or whoever, will just out of hand reject everything you suggest. In point of fact, when you write TV scripts one of the things young writers do is write stage directions into their script. Enter left. You know, tight shot here, close up, medium shot. The first thing your TV producer or director will do is just strike out all the directions. The director has got his own ideas of how he visualizes it. And he won't listen to the writer at all.

Q. Then the writer's story won't get on the screen as his own story, is that it? You may have heard Harlan Ellison talk about when he gets a story filmed sometimes he doesn't recognize it.

Bester: Yeah, sure, I understand that, but between Harlan and his director, Harlan has lost his clout. He's no longer in control. Once a script is written you're out of control. There's nothing you can do about it. You can't even cast it. You say to your director you see G. C. Scott as playing this part. He says 'Yeah, man, thanks very much,' and he casts Robert Cummings or someone like that. You're out of control, and you have to reconcile yourself to it and instead of sitting and beefing about it go and write another script. That's all.

Q. Might this not be what's wrong with Hollywood, why we get so many mediocre films?

Bester: No, what's wrong with Hollywood is that it's committee work. You know the old joke. What is a camel? A camel is a horse made by a committee. It's the committee work that is destructive. It was Kipling who said all work is one man's work, and that's perfectly true. One man's

15

work. Take Billy Wilder for example. From top to bottom he is in control of his films, from the writing through the casting, direction, everything else. Which is why his films are so great. One man's work.

Q. If you are a writer in Hollywood how do you beat that?

Bester: Oh, it's very simple. You don't go to Hollywood and you don't write in Hollywood. If I had a nickel for every offer I've turned down I could retire. No, I don't work on the coast because I can't stand the committee work. I have to be in control as much as possible. And since I am no better than my editor or my director, the only editors and directors I can work with are those who are intensely sympatico. If they think alike and see alike and hear dialogue the same way, then I know I'm safe. And these are the people I work with.

Q. Would you permit the filming of one of your novels?

Bester: Oh sure, all the novels have been under option for years. I know they'll never be made but what the hell do I care? I get a check every quarter for them and I stick the check in the bank and go out and buy books or buy booze or buy women. Whatever you can buy I buy with it. They'll never make them. It's all right with me.

Q. But suppose they did?

Bester: Well I wouldn't go to see it. Why should I?

Q. Thank you, Mr. Bester.

—Philcon, Dec. 1974

Robert Silverberg

Q. Science fiction has been accused of being, and at one time probably was, an entirely commercial product ground out by the yard, sort of like textiles. Yet today more writers are taking what they write seriously. How do you account for this shift away from formula fiction?

Silverberg: Well, I think it's part of a general change in American culture. All the arts—all the popular arts—have become incredibly more complex over the last twenty-five years. Just trace the evolution from Glenn Miller to Sgt. Pepper for example, and you see a picture of a whole other world in the sixties. SF was always a fairly complex literature of ideas even when it was just slam bang yardgood adventure stories on the surface. Content has met style and all that kind of noise. And in the course of the twenty-five year evolution of modern SF, which I think started somewhere after the war, we've reached an era of sophistication and complexity and perhaps even of decadence.

Q. You seem to have changed too. If you don't mind my saying so, didn't you start out as one of the by-the-yard people?

Silverberg: Oh I wrote tons—well let's stick to the yard analogy—well hundreds and hundreds of yards. Yeah, I was a kid right out of college and I was earning a living in the field of commercial fiction and I did not desire to rock the boat. I did what was necessary in order to earn my living, and at that time SF was a relatively limited field, limited artistically, limited financially, limited intellectually. As I grew up and as SF publishing grew up, we all changed, and I saw no point in continuing to turn out simple-minded commercial crap when I could be having a much more interesting time within my head writing the best work I could do.

Q. How did you go about it in those days? Wasn't Ziff Davis sort of legendary for doing it factory style?

17

Silverberg: I was part of the factory about 1955 or so when I was newly a professional. I was asked—I was invited—to contribute 50,000 words of fiction a month, in assorted lengths, anything from short stories to novelets, and I would receive a penny a word for this. That was a guaranteed $500 a month which is what most of my college classmates were making as engineers or draftsmen or whatever they were. Now the publisher of *Amazing* didn't care what his 50,000 words of stuff were as long as they looked like science fiction, had a robot in them here and there, the hero triumphed, and there was a lot of dialogue. I remember the editor saying "Put a lot of quotation marks in there. They really like quotation marks." This kind of publishing serves no human need that I know of except for the publisher's need to get his product on the newsstands once a month and the writer's need to pay his rent. Eventually it ceased serving any human need at all and it's no longer done, at least not in SF.

Q. Why do you think people read it?

Silverberg: A lot of people—SF is a schizophrenic field and always has been. It's an elitist field that has appealed to a sub-literate audience, an audience of boys and girls, mostly boys, in their teens, who cared more for fantastic ideas than for grammar and style, an audience of working class people who read it since their own childhood, but who had no great sophistication. People who thought of themselves as special, as an elite, because they read this strange, persecuted kind of fiction, but who were fairly close to illiterate. They were not particular about their science fiction. They couldn't get enough of it. It was an addiction. But today's readers, who by and large are college educated people, are a little more demanding. Today's society is more demanding.

Q. Were you more demanding than most when you were a reader yourself?

Silverberg: Oh yeah, I was a college boy and I would hang out with Kafka and Proust and then I would turn to *Amazing Stories* for fun, or for that mind-blowing particular thing which SF could occasionally give me then. And I had considerable contempt for those mass-produced factory magazines, and this of course involved some schizophrenia for me when I started writing for them. I simply separated my head from my fingertips, and the head could continue to read what it wanted to; the fingertips would produce $500 worth of junk a month. But that was all very long ago, and by the time I was twenty-eight or so I had outgrown that kind of very dangerous and destructive division of soul, and had decided; in fact I had no choice but to decide; to write only the kind of fiction which I would want to read. And that's my criterion now. I write stories which I would have wanted to read if somebody else had written them.

Q. In the beginning, didn't you aspire to write for the better magazines and in the manner of the better writers? Ziff Davis wasn't the top of the world, you know.

Silverberg: I certainly did. If I had had it in me to be Heinlein or Asimov or Vance, or whoever the current heroes were, I would have done it, but at the moment earning a living was more important. Also I wasn't Asimov or Heinlein; I was a twenty-one year old kid. And perhaps it was cowardly of me not to push myself to my limits then, but in fact my limits weren't very great. I'm not a twenty-one year old kid anymore and I have more to say, more things to share with my readers. I often wonder how my career would have worked out if I had always aimed for the best right from the very beginning. But the climate, the prevailing climate of publishing then did not encourage a writer to stretch himself, to expand himself, especially a young writer. It was very seductive to be told, "Hey come in and write some junk and I'll pay you enough to keep you eating." Today new young writers are sought out by editors and they're coddled and developed and their talents are shown to them, that they tend to make the best of themselves. I was led to make the worst of myself. The editors played to my weakest points, my own weaknesses of character, and it wasn't until I was twenty-five or so that I realized what was going on. And of course I was making a lot of money. I was winning economic independence by doing this, which was good because it's that economic independence which eventually allowed me to have artistic independence.

Q. How did you break out of this grind and start writing better stuff?

Silverberg: I got sick of the grind basically and I walked away from it. There was a big collapse of the SF magazine market. You must understand that SF was all magazines in the 1950s. Paperbacks and hardcover books were relatively insignificant as a market for writers. The magazines mostly went out of business. Those that remained reduced their rates. It became a very uncommercial thing and I figured if I'm going to sell my soul I'd better get a better price for it. So I drifted away from SF and then after writing a variety of odds and ends, anonymous fiction for almost anyone who would hire me, I began writing fairly serious non-fiction books on archeological subjects, working out of a private interest of my own. And though these too began out of the commercial orientation that I've always had, gradually they became very important to me and I found myself doing them seriously, doing them in a scholarly way, and suddenly I was somebody else. I had a new identity as a writer and I realized how much more I enjoyed working at the top of capacity instead of giving the least possible part of myself. By the time I'd spent ten years doing the archeological books and winning a pretty good reputation as a non-fiction science writer I had enough economic independence so that I could come back to SF, which in the meanwhile had changed tremendously for the better, and meet it on my own terms, and not make any concessions to any editor's idea of what SF ought to be.

Q. Now when you go about writing a story you're no longer paying the bills. What then are you doing? Getting a message across?

Silverberg: Well I like to say I'm making a verbal object. I'm making a thing out of words. Getting a message across—no, certainly that is not what I'm after. What I'm doing is for one thing exercising my gift. This is the one thing I do really well in the world and I certainly want to continue at it. And I'm putting down on paper a vision I want to record. What I think SF does uniquely is show the reader something he's never seen before, and only if a SF story does this is it worth anything to me. I wouldn't say this is the only criterion for a good SF story, but certainly it is for me. So if I see something, a bit of strangeness, I want to put it down on paper so it won't go away. So I write it down, and because I am a professional who understands the craft of shaping these things so they can be published, I put them out to be published.

Q. This thing you see, which no one has ever seen before, isn't it sometimes simply a view of ourselves from a different direction? I think I can cite an example, as what struck me as dealing with a contemporary problem from a good distance, and this is the section of *Tower of Glass* in which you can substitute "negro" for "android" and it still comes out coherent.

Silverberg: Yes, but that's the simplest level of *Tower of Glass*. It's so simple that I say it right in the book. It's the abolitionist movement all over again—let my people go. But there's a lot of other stuff going on in *Tower of Glass* having to do with the relationship of man to God and the relationship of synthetic beings to man, and fifty other things. It's a very complex book and it's one of my own favorites of my books for that reason. I threw so many things into it and I think I held them together. And also in *Tower of Glass* there are things which have only a private value to me, a line or two of description, a scene, a face, things which I see and I want to put down for my own reference. It's my good luck that the things I put down to amuse myself also interest others enough to pay to read them. So the social aspect of *Tower of Glass* is really just part of the structure, part of the thing I put there to hold the rest of it up. But it's such an obvious social point that I don't claim it has any importance in the book. I don't think slavery is very good, and so what?

Q. While we're talking about social points, how about the overpopulated society depicted in *The World Inside?* Was that intended to make a point or was it just a hypothetical society? Do you think we could possibly get from here to there?

Silverberg: Well, I don't think we can get specifically to that society; it's a very artificial society divided into people who live in highrise towers and people who live in farming communities and nothing in between, no suburbs. No, I don't think we'll ever get there. The story is more a parable than a forecast. I don't believe I can change society through my fiction. There is always social commentary because I put into a story what I see. I see the situation as deeply as I can and there are going to be social aspects and sexual aspects and sensory aspects. It's all part of the unified object I'm creating. That's why I reject the business of messages. I write about social problems because I write about people and whenever there's more than one of them in a room they have social problems. But I don't write warnings specifically. That's certainly not my motive though that may be the effect.

Q. Do you write anything you would consider serious speculation on the way you think the future really will turn out?

Silverberg: Yes, often, particularly in stories set in the near future. I try to be as realistic as I can within the basically visionary framework that I'm setting up. Certainly I think I was making a valid socio-economic point in *The World Inside*. In fact while I was in the process of making that point Paulo Soleri came along and made it in a much more visible way, with the idea that like it or not if we're going to increase our population we're going to move into a vertical society, a high rise society, so that we don't end up paving the entire earth. I was pleased with the idea when I thought about it, so I wound up putting it in the book. There are a lot of other things going on in that book which are more important to me as artist if not to me as political agitator.

Q. Then do you think that to you as an artist dealing with the relationship between man and God is more important than providing a Sears Catalogue of possible futures?

Silverberg: To me. There are many different kinds of SF and as a writer I am only interested in the kind of things I want to write. I always try and provide a plausible future, or almost always. A book like *Son of Man* which is simply a far-out trip, or not so simply a far-out trip, is of course not intended as a plausible speculation at all. But *The World Inside* is and in it I attempted to work out as carefully as possible how these things would work, how people would be shaped by life inside such a building, how I felt that such a society would come about from our society. I did the homework; I did the nuts and bolts of it, and I think this is part of a SF writer's responsibility, to make his vision as plausible as possible, but it is not necessarily a forecast. I am not in the business of prophecy.

Q. Do you then deliberately construct your work so that it'll last even if it doesn't come true? What would happen to *Dying Inside* if it were conclusively proven that there's no such thing as telepathy?

Silverberg: Well how do you arrive at a negative proof of anything? Yeah, I see what you mean. I think *Dying Inside* can be taken as a metaphor for loss regardless of what it is you're losing. In fact that's one of the criticisms the book has received, that it could have just as easily been about a master stud who is losing his virility, who can't get it up anymore. Well okay he can't get it up mentally. I make the same metaphor in the book. He thinks of his telepathy in terms of failing sexuality. But in fact I did write a book about telepathy and therefore in the science fictional parts of the book—the book is set in the very near future and a lot of it doesn't have a strong science fictional aspect—I attempted to get inside the nature of telepathy as well as I could and I'm very pleased

with what I achieved there, in conveying what it might be like to be tele-
pathic. And I've gotten some weird fan mail on that book from people
who say they are telepaths and 'you really got it right, fella' and it's just
scary to me.

Q. When you sit down to write a book, do you particularly worry whether or not it'll turn out as science fiction?

Silverberg: Well it always comes out SF in my head. That is, I believe
that the thing that I write is SF, but all I worry about when I sit down
to write the book is fulfilling whatever notion I had when I began the
book and the categories look after themselves. There's always some
strongly science fictional element in anything I write. In *Dying Inside*
there's telepathy. In *The Book of Skulls* there's immortality, and in my
new novel, *The Stochastic Man*, there's probability theory and precog-
nition. So even though my longer works seem to be slipping more and
more into very contemporary backgrounds, I still think of it as SF if I
think of it at all. Books like *Nightwings* or *Son of Man* or *Tower of Glass*
are obviously SF and I don't have to worry about the category at all.

Q. Do you find yourself typed as a category writer, or could you write
and sell a straight mainstream novel just as well?

Silverberg: Well I could sell it, but I don't know what would happen. I
feel most comfortable in science fictional ideas. That's where my natural
tendency lies. But I've never attempted, at least not in my ten years or
so as a fairly serious writer, to write a straight mainstream novel. I've
been sliding into mainstream apparently with things like *Dying Inside*
and *The Book of Skulls*. I don't know what would happen if I launched
a straight mainstream novel. However, I'm getting a bit of information
now about *Born With the Dead* which was published in a volume by
Random House not labelled science fiction at all, and it seems to be getting into bookstores in all sorts of strange places, occult, straight mainstream novel sections, and in the philosophical sections, even though
the bookstore clerks know me as a SF writer, and that's usually a draw-
back. So something may be changing there. I'll know more in about a
year.

Q. Do you think you'll be remembered and make an impression that
way? I've noticed that the survival rate seems to be much higher inside
the field than outside of it.

Silverberg: Well I'm only abstractly concerned with survival. I want
everybody to read and love my novels all over the planet and I want my
books to stay in print for hundreds of years after I die and all that, but
that's not very real to me. What's real to me is the day by day sweat of
getting the work done, and the pleasure of seeing it done. So I certainly
don't spend much time calculating how I can best survive down through
the ages, or how I can even survive beyond the end of this century as a
writer. If I could just go on earning royalties through my lifespan I'm
satisfied.

Q. Do you think that modern SF is going to be considered in the centuries to come as Literature with a capital L like the Bible and Shakespeare and all that? Do we have anything capable of doing that?

Silverberg: I don't think it's come along yet. It's very hard to have much perspective on the fiction of one's own time and talk about what's going to survive. I like to think that Faulkner, say, will survive, but I'm worried even about him, let alone Asimov and Heinlein and Lem and so forth. It would be good if something that is science fictional will survive. The only SF novel I can think of at the moment that has survived for any length of time is *Gulliver's Travels*, which to me is pure SF, and which seems to be immortal. Perhaps some of the great SF novels of our day will last into another century, perhaps *Brave New World* or *The Time Machine*. I really don't think there are many candidates for immortality among the Hugo winners. SF has not produced its Shakespeare and it may never.

Q. But is it possible?

Silverberg: I don't know. That's why I said 'and may never.' I'm troubled about SF as a lasting, overwhelmingly important artform, because many of its concerns are transient, so many of the problems and images we deal with are bypassed as time catches up with them. That is why I try to stay away from strict prophecy in my stories, because when you predict and predict wrongly your book has no life left in it. I'd rather work from absolutes if possible. And I just don't know. SF, though its history can be traced back to the *Odyssey* and what not, is really a very young field, and I haven't integrated in my own head its relationship to Sophocles and Shakespeare yet.

Q. Might that not be an advantage, that SF writers have at their disposal ideas, images, and even words which are not cluttered by four or five hundred years of literary usage? Don't we have more fresh material to work with and thus a better chance of lasting?

Silverberg: Well, when Homer did the *Odyssey* he had fresh material to work with. He threw the whole Mediterranean world populated with monsters and demons at us, and he's lasted quite well. Now we may do the same, but we're already getting cluttered with our own imagery, our own incestuous dependence on previous SF, and that worries me, that we will become hermetic and inaccessable to readers, because instead of dealing with archtypical mythic situations, we're dealing with the minutia of how to build a faster-than-light drive. And this I think may ultimately cook us eventually, the preoccupation with what is ultimately trivial.

Q. Might not the widely proclaimed possible fusion of SF with the mainstream prevent this? SF is reaching a much larger audience than ever before. Might that not tend to open things up and let a little fresh air in?

Silverberg: I think that if we write with the greatest intensity and richness at our command about situations that have the greatest possible emotional and intellectual power, we stand a pretty good chance of getting a hold on a large and enlightened audience. I'm not concerned with getting a large audience, *per se*. I have no intention of being Harold Robbins. I wouldn't mind making his money, but I don't want to do stuff that's so accessable that millions and millions of people all over the world read it, because all important fiction, all really powerful fiction, literary art, has been an elite art. I think that anything that is worthwhile is either folk art or elite art but nothing in between. The gray area of commercialism is useless and short-lived.

Q. Don't you think that the best literature of any kind works on all levels? Shakespeare was very popular with the common people of his day.

Silverberg: Is that true, or was he just speaking to the educated Londoners?

Q. They had a big hole in the ground below the stage in the Globe Theater which served as a low price seat. The nobility sat in the balconies, but the common people, or "groundlings" as they were called, also came and they did like the plays. The thing about Shakespeare is that he worked both on a superficial popular level and a more intellectual level.

Silverberg: Well, Dickens did that too, but sure you can write on many levels at once. I like to think that I do, but I don't think you can reach everybody at once. You can't be all things to all men. I'm not going to try.

Q. Thank you Mr. Silverberg.

—Discon II, Sept. 1974

Brian Aldiss

Q. What do you think would happen if we no longer had a recognizable category of science fiction, and everything was simply labelled "fiction?" How would this affect the situation of the reader and the writer?

Aldiss: I don't see what you mean, because it implies an entirely different standard of publishing. As I see it science fiction, among all the other things it is, is primarily a publisher's category, and you can't see them doing away with it. If you wanted a *hypothetical* category, then in a sense you're not looking forward; you're looking back to the time when people read science fiction and didn't know that's what it was called. The age of innocence, I suppose in many ways. I can see there might be advantages to that, in that you'd have to look much harder to find what you wanted, and you might find things that you weren't actually looking for that surprised you a lot. My idea of science fiction, science fantasy, etc., is that it always shades off into endless demarcations. You may have a hard-core center, but around it there's a whole area where definition is a lot more difficult. I believe that maybe it would help writers a lot more. I think the situation is different in the States from England, because over here, I believe, the boundaries are more rigidly set. In England the distributor is a less important figure in the publishing chain, so there's less insistence on whether it is science fiction or whether it's not. I'm not sure whether this hasn't influenced me in some way in my own writing. I've never much cared what it was as long as I've felt I was doing good, and I left it to the publisher after that to decide if he would put it out labelled science fiction or just as an ordinary novel with fantastic or prophetic elements.

Q. In your researches for *Billion Year Spree* you must have encountered some of those hundreds of 19th century science fiction novels that nobody reads anymore. Might it not be that these got lost in the great mass of general fiction and disappeared in their own day? They didn't have the science fiction label then.

Aldiss: Yes, I can certainly think of good examples like that. One's a book that has been reprinted fairly recently. It was originally called *Lieutenant Gulliver Jones, His Vacation* and it was reprinted by Ace Books as *Gulliver On Mars*. That was first published about 1905, and it simply died the death. And that was by a man who had also written two other fantasy novels. One, *Phra The Phoenician* is quite well known, a reincarnation novel. I think there's a good case that would support your point. Had there been a category then the man who wrote it, Arnold, would have found a readier audience. In fact what happened to him was he was disappointed by the lack of success of this book and he never wrote anything else. He would probably have been truly amazed to see *Phra The Phoenician* reprinted in the 1940s in *Famous Fantastic Mysteries,* amazed and I hope cheered to no end. And cheered to find *Gulliver On Mars* coming out. But I think you must also say that a lot of these novels were of their day, and had their day, and when the day's over they're really dead, perhaps not worth resurrecting. Worthy of archeology, maybe, but not of much interest today.

Q. What do you think makes a science fiction novel survive beyond its time?

Aldiss: I wish I knew the answer to that question. Some that seem to survive have an eternal thing about them, some sort of mythical quality. A lot that are reprinted today I find rather astonishing. For instance the William Morris titles, *The Well At The World's End*, this kind of thing. But that's not my favorite sort of a novel in any case. I think that they appeal to the reader who just wants to look beyond the present day. He wants to know about other civilizations and other cultures, and it may well be that old science fiction and fantasy does this in many cases even better than an ordinary straight novel geared to do that sort of thing.

Q. Today at the convention [Lunacon 1975] Sam Moskowitz tried to refute the claim you made in *Billion Year Spree* that *Frankenstein* was the first recognizable science fiction novel. He then talked about a twenty-five novel science fiction anthology published in the 18th century, and several other things. What have you to say about that?

Aldiss: Well, it's a case of insistence really, with everybody putting forth their viewpoints. There's a very arguable viewpoint that *Frankenstein* has all the recognizable ingredients of a science fiction novel, and that it's the first one to have those, and you can readily identify those elements. I think they're important. I don't honestly think that Sam has got a good counter-argument. The great thing about *Frankenstein* is that Frankenstein creates life, and this is an example of an entirely unprecedented invention. Moreover, he creates this without any form of supernatural aid. Incidentally, I think he's a very interesting paradigm of an inventor, in that having created he is not interested in the control, and that is left to society. And well we know all about that, and this is what has made the *Frankenstein* theme a very up to date theme, and worth a

26

bit more consideration than being made into horror movies. Really the essential point of *Frankenstein* which Mary Shelley saw very clearly in 1818, was that it was no use appealing to old authority. Victor Frankenstein in his research is looking at thousand year old authors. He's reading Paracelaus, Cornelius Agrippa, Galen, and so on. And he's getting nowhere, and it's only when he's at the university that they say to him, "Oh throw that away. These are men who promised everything and delivered nothing. Go to modern research and see what's being done under the microscope and in the crucibles." This I think is *absolutely* crucial to science fiction. I don't see any gainsaying it. It's one thing to argue that there was no immediate followup from this, but that's neither here nor there. The fact is that Mary Shelley was ahead of her time in this recognition, and so that it's only later that it seems to be followed up. But that doesn't disprove it as seminal science fiction. It merely shows that it was seminal science fiction. The other argument of course, about the origins of science fiction, is that it goes much earlier than the last century. Now there you get in very deep water, because there you're going to start talking about second century Greeks, and endless voyages to the Moon transported there by flying birds or ill winds. You're going to find yourself talking about Dante's *Inferno*, Shakespeare's *Tempest*, the *Epic of Gilgamesh*, the first chapter of *Genesis*, and all that sort of thing. And my answer to this is that well, yes, these have certain special qualities about them that seem to have something in common with perhaps the catastrophe novel in science fiction, but in fact the boot is on the other foot, and SF has taken over as its subject a lot of the subjects that once belonged to other sorts of literature. Another example which people readily comprehend is that science fiction has taken over some of the material of Daniel Defoe's *Robinson Crusoe*. Essentially Crusoe's desert island is another planet. It's interesting that there actually was a novel called *No Man Friday* by Rex Gordon, which I think in the States was called *Robinson Crusoe on Mars*.

Q. Yes, they made a film out of it.

Aldiss: That's right, they did it without paying a single dime to Rex Gordon, I understand. *Robinson Crusoe* is part of the essence of science fiction. *Gulliver's Travels* has its satirical method to deal with longevity and strange races, and so on. But this is not to say that these are true science fiction. Maybe they're forerunners of science fiction, but science fiction has come along, and in its avid search for method and subject matter, it has subsued all these subjects into the body of its discussion.

Q. You'll notice that a lot of the writers are very cautionary, and often they're opposed to change. They show what will happen if such and such is invented and it's always bad. Do you think this is a result of the influence of *Frankenstein?*

Aldiss: Well, I would want to think about that point, but I certainly take your glancing reference that many science fiction writers *do* seem adverse to change. Ray Bradbury of course is a good example, and it's interesting to see that science fiction writers are not on the whole a body of men who support any changes in the direction of science fiction. They are, I think, surprisingly conservative in their views. On the other hand you could oppose them to men like Philip K. Dick. I think in Dick's work you see something like Bradbury's fascination with the past, but Dick I think always sees it as a trap. This is one thing that makes me admire Dick's work so much, that throughout his novels are scattered characters who have recreated worlds that they can live in, and they're always dead worlds. However terrible Dick's futures may be, he sees it as something less dreadful than the past, I think. Maybe at the present moment things have changed. Science fiction, after all, is responsive as a thermometer to changes in the socio-economic state of the world, and in the Gernsback epoch, in the twenties and thirties, despite the depression, those were great expansionist books, bursting out into the galaxy. It was the way mankind felt about technology, that it would get us through all the evils and misfortunes that were still in society. Now, sadder, wiser, we see that technology always brings its own complications, and that behind technology is a human society, man himself, an aspiring but mixed up creature. So I think modern science fiction is more skeptical. A lot more sophisticated perhaps, but more skeptical.

Q. Do you find modern science fiction writers conservative in a literary sense?

Aldiss: No, I don't. I should have thought that there was a change in the 1960s in the literary sense in that they were much more interested in exploring freer forms and taking the thing apart to see what they could do. I'm a great believer myself in having a beginning, a middle, and an end in a story, if not in that order. I like a story—I like a narrative. But there were a number of writers who thought it would be a very good idea to have a non-linear narrative. I think that perhaps a lot of those experiments were abortive, as they always are, but a lot of them were useful to the writers concerned, and perhaps to the writers coming afterwards. In England in particular we had a very good mix. The sixties was a very fluid time. The arts were mixed up a great deal, with all sorts of art forms, visual media, television, radio and so on. And this really opened things up in England. It brought science fiction there a very much larger audience. I think an equivalent happened in the States, but well I'm not very qualified to speak about that.

Q. But didn't all this experimentation prove disastrous for *New Worlds* magazine?

Aldiss: Well, *New Worlds* was the sort of laboratory where a lot of it took place, but I don't think that was the reason why *New Worlds* in the end was disastrous. It was simply that *New Worlds* had lost a publisher for many years, had lost a printer. Well, as Alfie Bester once said, you should go for broke. And *New Worlds* certainly went for broke, and in the end it broke. But in that period I think that among the dross you can pick out good things that happened, Disch's *Camp Concentration*, Spinrad's *Bug Jack Barron*, a lot of J. G. Ballard's stories. I suppose you might include my own *Barefoot In The Head*.

Q. It seems to me that what happened at the very end was they lost interest in publishing science fiction, and lost their audience accordingly.

Aldiss: Well, I wouldn't really like to comment on that. Looking at what *New Worlds* has become now I think you have a strong case for saying that.

Q. Well, I have a theory that you can get away with slipping quantities of non-science fiction material in something labelled science fiction and the reader won't protest, but there's a breaking point at about forty percent. *New Worlds* went well over.

Aldiss: Yes, this happens from time to time. When Sturgeon was a known name in his early years, he could always write a story which really had nothing to do with science fiction or anything to do with fantasy, and still it would be published in a science fiction magazine simply because it was Sturgeon and the interest was there. That was very much the way it was at *New Worlds*. A sort of dare went on to see what you could do next and the excitement was in following it. And the excitement in any magazine was that it must have a powerful motivation and the readership follows those things. And this is what happened with *Astounding* under John W. Campbell in the '40s. I think it's important to see just how far you can carry science fiction in those directions. In fact this is the whole history of science fiction's contemporary success, I think, that it now covers a much wider field than it did in the early '50s.

Q. I notice that a lot of the extreme stuff in the late *New Worlds* was just somebody fooling around with style without having any interesting content. Now they don't do that anymore, so whatever happened to the "new wave?"

Aldiss: Well, again I say, I think that science fiction is a very sensitive thermometer to the state of society, and that society itself has changed a great deal. It's like saying, well okay the Beatles broke up, so the Beatles were no good. I think this is the implication behind your question. And this isn't so. The Beatles were very good in their time, but they reached their limit and I think it was the same way with *New Worlds*. I haven't got much sympathy for *New Worlds* at the moment, but I don't think that denigrates what it did in the past.

Q. What did we get of lasting value from all that?

Aldiss: Well, I think I've briefly sketched it in. There were certain things that it seems will last, that people have accustomed themselves to. The extraordinary thing was that people were so reluctant to go along with any sort of experimentation. Well, if an art form has no experimentation, you know as well as I do that it does. So what I think happened then was an infusion of life.

Q. What do you think caused all the furor? Do you remember the "new wave" flap of about 1966-70? Was this caused just by an injection of literate prose, or what?

Aldiss: No, I think it was just that people were not accustomed to these things. They were just startled. A lot of people adapted to it. Again I can't speak for the States, but in England *New Worlds* brought a whole lot of new readers into reading science fiction. They suddenly saw a magazine that was clearly of its time and wasn't some sort of old fossil or dinosaur. And they went for that, and it was very successful. You know, they bring in new readers just the way *Star Trek* brings in new readers. All these things enlarge the field. No one reader has to like all of it, but by God you'd better acknowledge that it's there.

Q. What condition did you find the field in when you entered it?

Aldiss: Well, again I suppose—from my own experience—I found that there was no sense at all that I was being other than absolutely mad to go for science fiction. There was very little of it being published, and most of it was an American product, and I know a lot of well informed, well meaning people who tried to dissuade me, and said "What are you writing this stuff for? It won't give you any literary rewards. It won't give you any financial rewards." And for a few years that seemed to be so, but nevertheless I felt that I was a science fiction writer. That was what I wanted to write in the main. Well, all I can say is that things changed. I think that I was among those people who helped change it, and notably because in the early '60s I edited the Penguin science fiction anthologies. They were best sellers of the Penguin list and they served to introduce all sorts of American writers to England who had never been published over there before. I actually met one or two of those authors at this convention who came up to me and said, "Mr. Aldiss, you're the first person who ever anthologized me." Well, that's good, and you hear that news fifteen years later and it still feels good. I did a lot of that. Then the BBC did a television series of science fiction stories, and a lot of those stories they took straight and direct from my Penguin anthologies. You have to ask Philip K. Dick, Alan Nourse, people like that. They'll tell you.

Q. Who were the people who first gave you big breaks, possibly in reverse by publishing you in the United States?

Aldiss: Well, I owe a great debt to many people, in particular to Heinlein, whose "Universe" I loved. My first novel, known as *Starship* over here, was in a way a direct response to that. I thought there were all sorts of important things he'd left out, emotional things which I put in. Again that's part of the continuing dialogue of the field over the years, the really great, good thing about science fiction, I think, that it always goes on with this continuing dialogue. The characters may change, but we're all built up on what was there before. I also owe a lot to Fred Pohl who published my first story over here, and to Anthony Boucher, and in particular to a man at New American Library, Truman Talley who took over all my early books from Faber, my English publisher, published them well, put on good covers, distributed them well. In fact my early reputation was over here, and not in my own country. It was only later that the science fiction field opened up in Great Britain. And there I suppose I owe a lot to people like Kingsley Amis, who always spoke out for science fiction, and Angus Wilson, and the people who helped to see that science fiction was received on a good cultural level.

Q. Until recently science fiction was something that was sneered at in the United States. Was it more respectable in England?

Aldiss: Well, it was sneered at in England. Since we had less of it anyhow, we had less of the bottom of the barrel than you did among other things. But don't forget that we have a long and honorable succession of writers who have always been well regarded and who have written science fiction without it necessarily being regarded as such. And I mean the tradition with, well, Mary Shelley, Wells, Aldous Huxley, Olaf Stapledon, George Orwell, this sort of thing. Also people like E. M. Forster or Rudyard Kipling who have written science fiction and fantasy stories. So I think on the whole it was received more readily at what you call a "critical" level.

Q. Might it not be that science fiction wasn't ghettoized into a pulp category as it was over here?

Aldiss: Well, we didn't have the pulps. That was for sure. We had a lot of magazines but pulps was purely an American term, a technical term for the paper, and whether or not that made a difference I don't know. Maybe it did.

Q. I might also point out that the early British science fiction magazines do not have scantily clad maidens being chased by octopuses all over the covers. They usually had tasteful covers that had something to do with the contents.

Aldiss: Well, I have a nostalgia actually for scantily clad girls pursued by scantily clad octopuses. In fact I've just finished putting together a book on science fiction art, which includes interiors and cover illustrations from the old magazines. My feeling is that although there were the Earle Bergey covers, nevertheless the standard was pretty good and pretty startling, and will be recognized as such. I think the pulps did good.

Q. Well, it got to the point that these covers were a trademark and they were just slapped on, without any control from the editor. This didn't happen in Britain, which would mean the marketing was different.

Aldiss: Well, that's true. It was on a more amateur basis, I think, but also we didn't have the same circumstances. One thing I think that was dangerous about the pulps was that they had a tendency toward monoculture. That is to say one magazine was devoted to one very narrow and specific genre, such as sea stories, railroad stories, ranch stories,

31

G-men stories, ad infinitem. Science fiction stories. In England you had fewer magazines and they stayed in what you might call the primitive state, like the *All Story* magazine or *Argosy*. They would put a whole gamut of stories in. I suppose that accounts for some of the differences between the two countries.

Q. You'll notice that between the middle '20s and the middle '40s there was no science fiction book publishing in the United States. How did it happen in England? Was there a book market in that period?

Aldiss: Well, yes, certainly, the great epoch of the hardcover book, but there was very little science fiction. I would guess that anyone who looked on themselves as science fiction writers *per se* would be contributing to the American pulps. People like John Wyndham in his early days as John Beynon Harris, and John Russell Fearn under all his multitudinous pen-names—I think 32 recorded to date. These people would see their market in the States. And so it began.

Q. At what point did you start reading science fiction?

Aldiss: Well, there were several points, and it's hard for me to distinguish really. I read H. G. Wells novels very early, although it wasn't until later that I actually appreciated them. I came across the pulps when I was about 12, because Woolworth's in England used to sell old pulps. That was when I first encountered *Amazing,* which I thought was dreadful but I was fascinated by it. And *Astounding* which I found baffling but I was still fascinated. And, I read Edgar Allan Poe, who was always very popular in England, and in particular a novel called *The Strange Invaders* by a Welshman called Llewellyn, and that persuaded me that you could actually write these marvellous things and write them well. It was a beautifully written book. That was the one that didn't just turn me on to reading but made me think that perhaps I'd like to write something like that, although I was a kid at the time. And then I had gone on to *Astounding.* They had stopped running Doc Smith. I couldn't read Doc Smith.

Q. Were the first attempts at writing you made science fiction?

Aldiss: Well I remember writing science fiction when I was six or eight or something like that, so you couldn't say I'm particularly new to the idea. I seem to have been writing it before I actually knew that it existed, which was rather odd.

Q. When did you get to the point where you thought you actually could make a career out of it?

Aldiss: Well, that was rather odd really, because I came to a point where I found that writing spare time was earning as much as my nine to five job, and at that point the logic of the situation seemed to dictate that I should march into the office and say, "Well friends it's been swell, but bye." And I walked out and that was it. I gave myself a year to make good, and in those days making good meant earning about 600 pounds. Then you could keep yourself and your family. So I wrote two novels that year, neither of which were accepted, and I was in trouble, but I wrote some short stories and they sort of bailed me out. Pride forbad that I should go back to my job, so I starved for a bit, and then suddenly the two novels were both accepted and other things were coming on, and so the bacon was saved. And from then on the situation has been, well, not too difficult. In fact progressively easier I would say.

Q. I know you have expanded into doing straight fiction, but have you ever gone beyond that? Have you ever tried to write for films?

Aldiss: Well, I would never try to write for films. If they invited me then I'd think hard about it, but I did have one brush with the film world which wasn't too fortunate. Interesting and amusing and exciting, but not too fortunate. Well, I'll wait till they come to me. I'm not particularly interested in anything else. I write a little poetry. I've done an awful lot of criticism in one form or another. Of course then I've had great success with straight novels which are very English and don't transpose too well to other countries. The nice thing about writing science fiction is that it is a sort of international language. Your books are translated into the main world language, and so you can pop up in Tokyo and people will say, "Oh hi Brian, I enjoyed your last book." That's a nice feeling.

Q. What do you have coming up now?

Aldiss: I've got three books coming up, two of which are signed, sealed, and more or less delivered, and they're delights. One is the book of science fiction art, and that's been nice because I've been working in pictures really instead of words and that will appear from Crown publishers in the States about early fall. And then I also have a volume which will be published on the first of May (1975) in England called *Hell's Cartographers* which is memoirs by six science fiction writers, of My Life and Times. That's really a good book. That's got Bob Silverberg, Damon Knight, Alfie Bester, Fred Pohl, and my co-editor and my old friend Harry Harrison, and myself also doing our stuff. That's a good book. And then I have a very long work of fiction of which the first draft is complete but I won't say anything about that because it'll take a few more months before I get that in shape. Oh, and a series of anthologies. I'm still working away introducing American writers to England and possibly vice-versa.

Q. Are you in general pleased with the way your career has gone and what you have written?

Aldiss: Oh I don't think you can answer that. Yes, I've been very fortunate in many ways. At the same time you're never quite satisfied with what you've done. Sometimes it works out right and you think, "God, this time some of the vision got through." But at other times I feel that it didn't. I don't know, I think you're right to be dissatisfied, really.

You see I've never been a great producer. The science fiction field is full of great producers who wind up as pretty burnt out cases at the age of forty. I never succumbed to that temptation. With each novel I feel that I'm beginning again. You know. Life's great age begins anew.

Q. Thank you, Mr. Aldiss.

—Lunacon, April 1975

James Gunn

Q. Science fiction has suddenly gotten very respectable. How would you account for that?

Gunn: Well, a lot of things have suddenly gotten very respectable. This is actually sort of a pop culture era, when a great many things which have occurred relatively without academic notice have suddenly had a great deal of interest in the academic area. One example of this which isn't often thought of is American Studies, which came into the university curriculums about 15-20 years ago, perhaps a little longer than that in some places. But it was followed up by the popular culture movement which had a number of manifestations. There was the pop art which made art out of soupcans and other kinds of materials found around us in everyday life. There was the pop music which began to come into curriculums in part through the respectability of jazz and through the recognition of other kinds of musicians. I remember Leonard Bernstein doing a television show five or six years ago in which he was praising the musicianship of the Beatles. So SF is following a general trend in which the pop lit, pop arts, are receiving attention, in part because students are interested in them, in part because people who once enjoyed them are now wanting to teach them, and to bring them into conjunction with the academic institutions, and in part because of a certain vitality within science fiction itself. Or to put it another way, a certain lack of vitality in certain aspects of mainstream literature.

Q. Do you think that putting SF in the classroom will have the same effect that putting mainstream fiction in the classroom did?

Gunn: I don't think—when I talk about mainstream literature I'm talking about Hemingway and Faulkner; I'm talking about popular contemporary writers like John Updike, Philip Roth, and others. I don't think they've diminished their stature or diminished their popularity. If any-

35

thing I suspect that they have enhanced those writers, that more people have read them, more people than would have if they had not been brought into the academy. If one looks back at certain other popular writers, like Shakespeare for instance, who was a popular writer of his day, the fact indeed that we still can read Shakespeare, that we can still see Shakespeare plays, is a product of the fact that he was recognized over the years as having something to say to us. And if indeed he had not been so recognized by the academy it's unlikely that today anyone would be conscious of Shakespeare.

Q. Do you think then that teachers form the literary tastes of the masses? If everybody studies science fiction in high school and college, will that vastly increase the readership for it?

Gunn: I think it will. Not because of the teachers' forming popular taste; it will increase the readership of science fiction because young people who would not have found it otherwise are going to be exposed to it and they're going to enjoy it, and they're going to go on and read other things. One example I might give you is when I taught my first science fiction class at the University of Kansas, some four years ago, the college bookstore suddenly had a run on science fiction criticism. They happened to have been knowledgeable about the matter, but they said "We're selling out of those Advent books on science fiction criticism, and it must be your class that's responsible," and I'm sure it was. There was interest in not only the reading of science fiction, but they wanted some comment about it as well.

Q. You mean you didn't assign those books?

Gunn: No, they just went out and got them themselves.

Q. Is the general reader interested in criticism?

Gunn: Well, what is fandom but a kind of criticism? The general reader reads fan magazines, reads criticism. Well, the first thing I turn to in a science fiction magazine, long before I read the magazine itself, is its reviews. I don't know how many other people do that. Maybe it's my own particular interest, but I suspect that many people are interested in what a reviewer has to say about contemporary SF.

Q. These attitudes are certainly prevalent among the very active readers, but then fandom comprises at best ten percent. Do you think that the general reader, the average college student, is going to be interested in real science fiction scholarship?

Gunn: I don't think he'll be all that interested in scholarship. Some of them will, some of them won't. It depends upon the depth of their interest. Some will read some of it and enjoy it and go on to read more. Others will be turned off by science fiction. But at least they'll be exposed to it and have an opportunity to be turned on by it.

Q. Now when you are teaching a science fiction course, how do you go about it, what do you do in the classroom?

Gunn: Well, you want to approach SF in a lot of different ways. I happen to teach it from a historical viewpoint. It's my conviction that a reader cannot really appreciate contemporary science fiction unless he knows how it got to be contemporary SF. And so I try to trace the evolution of science fiction, what made it what it is, through the study of certain historical trends, sociological, technological, and scientific influences, which eventually produced over a period of a couple of centuries, what we know as science fiction.

Q. How does your being a teacher of science fiction affect you as a writer? Do you find this very compatible or does it take up writing time, or what?

Gunn: Well, there's no doubt that whatever you do takes up time you could be using for writing. At the same time I should say that being a teacher gives me some freedom to write only what I'm really interested in writing, and that which I think is worth writing, rather than what might sell. There are many people who are full-time science fiction writers who turn out work not because it is particularly what they want to write, but because it is what they know they must write in order to meet the bills. Fortunately having another kind of job, which I like very much, teaching, gives me the opportunity to be very choosy about what I want to write, and it is true as well that the academic scene provides, and in fact expects me to do this kind of work. It is part of my responsibility as a teacher of fiction writing and as a teacher of science fiction, to be creative in this area.

Q. Then if every science fiction writer had another job to support him, wouldn't the quality of the field as a whole go up?

Gunn: Everybody's different; you can't generalize from one person's experience for everybody. I think for some people the discipline of full-time writing is essential. I did write full time for a period of 4 years and if it hadn't been for certain circumstances I might be freelancing now. But for some of us, a few of us, having a compatible job like this gives us a certain advantage. Some people, I suspect maybe Phil Klass is one of them [better known by his pseudonym *William Tenn*] find all their energies going into teaching and do very little writing. Others like myself are able to adjust to these different demands and spend energies both ways. I might say also that it seems to me that perhaps teaching brings a different quality to writing as well. When one is teaching literature one becomes conscious of certain values that can be found in writing, which one would like to put in one's own writing. So it may be that my writing has become a little denser, a little more multi-leveled than it once was, or perhaps this is merely due to the effect of experience and maturity, which allows me to focus on those things which I might not have done without teaching.

Q. So a writer who has time to work is going to produce a work of vastly greater depth than the bulk of writers, than any freelancer?

Gunn: Well, let's take one example for instance. For John Brunner the writing of *Stand on Zanzibar* [Hugo Award winner 1968—the ultimate overpopulation novel] was a very serious economic risk. He was only able to do it because a publisher was willing to advance him a considerable sum of money, having confidence in his ability to do this kind of work for which they could get back their advance, because John had to spend many more months on this book than he would have had to spend on any of the other books he writes. This sort of decision would not have been difficult for me. I would have been willing to spend the time necessary to produce the book if I could have written it—wish I had— because I do not have the economic pressure to keep producing work, to produce that which is easily saleable.

Q. Now that we are getting writers to take a chance, are we generally better off than we were twenty years ago when the field was more commercial? Are we presently living in the golden age of science fiction?

Gunn: Oh, I think there are. . . It's a matter of psychological viewpoint. The golden age is usually when one starts reading science fiction, because those are the stories which turn you on to science fiction and they have that aura of newness and the miraculous. There are a lot of exciting things going on, but I'm not sure at the moment whether they are of enduring value, and it remains to be seen. Only the future can look back on the present and say this was a golden age.

Q. Well, what do you have—what do you think will survive now? Any type and particular writer? What will become real classics?

Gunn: Well, I think some writers, some works will become classics. I think Ursula Le Guin's *The Left Hand of Darkness* is one, and perhaps Frank Herbert's *Dune* is another. And perhaps *Stand on Zanzibar*, perhaps Robert Silverberg's *Dying Inside*. And there are many others. And the thing that sets these books apart is that they are primarily experimental. They're primarily statements of mature writers who are now writing at the top of their form, who are trying to do something more ambitious than they tried to do before, and I think they are succeeding, because obviously they have been recognized as broadly as writing something of exceptional merit.

Q. Well, when you write a book, such as, say, *The Listeners*, what are you trying to do?

Gunn: Well, I was trying to write as good a novel as I could. But mainly I was trying to attempt something different. The general subject appealed to me. The image I suppose, of people listening to voices from the stars, because it is a striking image. It gets back really to quite a basic dichotomy with man's hopes for the universe. The one hope for instance, that we are the chosen, the elect, the only sentient creatures, the only ones favored by God and the universe, and we are alone. The other is the hope that we are not alone, that there are other people, other creatures intelligent enough to communicate with us, to share our dreams that we can share ideas and cultures with them. Just as in part of *The Listeners* I refer to the old problem of the human imagination, both in imagining a universe without a beginning or end, or imagining a beginning to the universe and wondering what existed before that. Both of them are basic, contradictory images. They chase out the other one. Neither one of them is completely consistent, and out of this, I hoped to make *art*, a story people would want to read, about the basic problem, not only in the physical terms of listening for voices from the stars, but as well the basic problem between the individuals, between humans, communications at all levels. I tried to pair off the problems of interstellar communication with those of interhuman communication.

Q. Another place where you got in front of a large audience, aside from your books, was a television show based on *The Immortal*. Did you have a hand in that show and did you approve of what they did?

Gunn: No. I had no hand in it. I sold the motion picture and TV rights to the book, and although I did have a little bit of influence with the scriptwriter who did the original motion picture of the week, which preceded the series by a year, I did not have any influence on the series itself. If you have read my *TV Guide* article on the subject you'll know that I thought it was pretty poorly done as a series. It sacrificed any SF value it might have, any appeal of the ideas, except for the basic concept of personal immortality which can be passed on to other people—sacrificed all those potentials in order to make another adventure show, another *Fugitive*.

Q. Do you think it was necessary to simplify sophisticated science fiction concepts for a mass audience? The producer certainly did.

Gunn: No, I don't think it's true. I think that's a misconception on the part of the people who are in charge of making decisions like this, and I think that upon occasion, when the producers have not underestimated the intelligence or the appreciation of the audience they have come up with something which has been top rated and excellently done. For instance the Jacques Cousteau undersea specials, the works which have appeared on public broadcasting, the various series from England, the *Upstairs, Downstairs*, the *Civilisation* series, for that matter those which appeared on public television, the Alastair Cook's *America* series. Everytime something has been done with taste and intelligence I think it has been successful.

Q. Has anything been done with taste and intelligence in the science fiction field? Or is the first adult SF series yet to come?

Gunn: Not consistently. I have seen a few shows that would—that I would have sat down and read as books. Certainly *Star Trek* had its moments, but they were not consistent and they were tied to a formula.

There were occasional good shows on the science fiction and fantasy anthology shows back in the time when they were doing such things. But on the whole there has been nothing at which one can point and say, "This is outstanding science fiction."

Q. Have you had any other brushes with the visual media aside from *The Immortal?*

Gunn: I had a story called "The Cave of Night" that was made into an hour television show on the old *Desilu Playhouse* back in 1959. It was a good production with E. G. Marshall and Lee Marvin but unfortunately they missed the whole point of the story.

Q. Have you ever done screenwriting yourself?

Gunn: I have done some screenwriting, and one of my screenplays, or my one screenplay which was an adaptation of my story "The Reluctant Witch" came within a hair of being made into a movie. Actually they had started shooting when suddenly the money they were counting on didn't show up.

Q. So it was never produced at all?

Gunn: No.

Q. What do you have coming up in the future? Do you have any irons in the fire?

Gunn: I might mention that *The Listeners* has been optioned for television or movies; I don't know which way they'll go. And there is some hope that perhaps something might be done with this. I have a new book just out called *Some Dreams Are Nightmares* from Scribner's, a new book coming up next year from Scribner's *The End of The Dreams.* My history of science fiction called *Alternate Worlds* will be published by Prentiss-Hall a year from now. I have two more books coming out from Scribner's, two additional books from those mentioned. *The Listeners* will be out in paperback from New American Library in October. I'm working on a novel for Bantam Books called *Kampus.* This is my major effort at the moment.

Q. Well, for a part-time writer you seem rather active.

Gunn: Yes, I suddenly got a lot of contracts all at once, and some of these books are previously written in part and aren't too difficult to put together. Some of them I'm working very hard on.

Q. Thank you, Mr. Gunn.

—Discon II, September 1974

Gardner Dozois

Q. Tell me, why did you become a writer rather than get an honest job? Do you think writers are born that way?

Dozois: Actually I became a writer because I'm lazy; I think most writers are lazy. I hate 9-5 jobs. They grind me down with boredom after a while. I'd rather live in relative poverty on my own time than try and hack working for somebody else, which I don't find very enjoyable. Writers can sit around with their eyes closed pretending they're plotting out stories, and as long as the snores coming out aren't too loud, then people will usually let them get away with it. So I think there is a certain amount of laziness in one respect of being a writer. In another respect just about any straight job I've ever had has bored the shit out of me eventually. So maybe it's not interesting enough after you've been a writer, especially a writer of something as wild as science fiction, where there's a lot of intellectual and creative excitement involved in doing what you're doing. A lot of regular jobs seem rather pale by comparison.

Q. Why did you turn to science fiction?

Dozois: I don't know. I think I basically got into SF when I was a kid, because SF was such a despised, underdog type of literature and I was such a despised underdog type of kid that there was sort of a natural affinity. This has changed a lot, like today SF is more respectable. On the college campus and in the highschools it's very popular. It's almost the in thing to read SF, almost like a brownie point to read SF. But when I was a kid things were entirely different. If people found out you read science fiction they looked at you in horror as if you had lice or ringworm or the clap or something. If you were unwise enough to be seen reading an SF mag or book on a subway or a bus people would give you odd looks and glance at you in disgust. The school librarian at my highschool used to frown very menacingly at me every time I took

41

out a new Robert Heinlein juvenile or something, and shake their heads. Today people are doing masters theses on science fiction, but in those days. . . I tried to do a paper in highschool on science fiction. I got a flat flunking grade and a nasty remark that science fiction was not a fit topic for literary evaluation. But all this sort of engendered a sympathy, a sort of forbidden fruit type thing. My parents used to forbid me to read science fiction; I used to smuggle it into the house and hide it the way people hide grass today. And I think that definitely had an effect, but as well as that what I said about working applies. I found most other forms of literature to be rather boring. I think the magic, the lure of mystery and distance and far horizons was what originally drew me into science fiction.

Q. Well, where do you think science fiction is going to take you as a writer?

Dozois: As a writer, probably to the poorhouse. SF is still a very low paying field. This is because as a genre it ducked into the pulp magazines back in the '30s and became ghettoized as a sort of substandard literature for morons and perverts and as a result there has been a long tradition of paying rock bottom prices to science fiction writers.

Q. Do you think this will improve in the future?

Dozois: Well, I think it'll gradually get a little bit better, because everything is getting more expensive. They're going to have to raise the price a little bit eventually, but I still think that for the next few years at least science fiction writers as a group will probably be on the bottom of the pay scale.

Q. Where do you think science fiction as a literature is going?

Dozois: Well, this gets into a very blurry area, because there are quite a few mainstream writers of note who are starting to dabble around in science fiction. I remember there was a book called *The Throne of Saturn* by Allan Drury which was a novel about the first flight to Mars and it was something like five or six hundred pages long. Now this would be a joke within genre science fiction because the material has been worked over so many times, everything has been said so much more concisely before. Still Drury was probably paid ten times as much for his book as most science fiction writers will ever get for theirs. Now I don't know whether this will eventually end up in earning more money for the genre science fiction writers or not. I think a lot of this depends on how well science fiction continues to sell. It's selling very well among "young people" and "counterculture" people right now. The college market is the big plum that all the publishers are snapping after. And if it continues to sell well, like for the next five or six years, I think that there may be a general elevation in prices and distribution and all the other things that hold it down.

Q. How do you think science fiction compares to the mainstream today in respects to quality?

Dozois: In respects to quality. . . Well, it's kind of hard to compare them because in some ways they're doing two different things. In the first place I think most straight mainstream literature, in other words about 70% of the fiction books that come out, really don't do much of anything at all. I don't think they really have much relevancy to the world we live in or to the way it's changing or to the things that affect us as people and as human beings. They don't. . . they just don't have any application to today's world. Now I think there's a branch of mainstream fiction, the avant-garde fiction that you find in, for instance, *The New American Review* and the little literary magazines that gives you some insight into what today's world is like and where we're going and how we're changing, but it does it in a very poetic way, it gives you the emotional side, how it feels where we're going, how it feels to be there, how it's going to feel when we get there, but it usually doesn't tell us in hard practical intellectual terms what is going to happen or what it's going to be like when we get there. I think this is what a lot of SF does. It does tell us what is going to happen in the intellectual sense rather than in the emotional sense that you get from avant-garde fiction. Now hopefully the best of science fiction is combining the 2 processes where you get a story that not only tells you what is going to happen in the future but how it feels, how it's going to feel and how it's going to affect us. I think that's the potential strength of science fiction, the ability to mold magic and intellect, sort of a synthesis between the emotion and the mind, or the intellectual reality.

Q. This is a rather general question, but where do you think we are going as a race? Do you think we have any chance?

Dozois: Sometimes I think the future will be called on account of rain. But I see several general futures for humanity, and it's really hard to say at this point where we're going to go. The future wherein we either blow ourselves to bits or strangle in our own excretia and end up dying pretty much in every root and branch—that's one. There's the future wherein we don't quite get to the point where humanity dies out completely; either some natural disaster or series of inevitable system failures will drop us back several hundred years to a less industrialized level and we'll start the whole shebang all over again. Then, three, if we manage to avoid those two, there's the future where somehow we manage to survive without strangling ourselves to death and technology keeps on increasing at the same breakneck pace that it has for the last 50 years and things just get stranger and stranger. Most of your SF deals with these three general futures. The 3rd future is the most interesting from a fictional standpoint. There's not really much to say about a future wherein everybody dies of pollution once you've said that everybody is going to die of pollution. But assuming as a postulate that we can somehow get by the crunch that's coming up in the next twenty or thirty years and technology does keep advancing, there is lots of weird stuff coming up. . . genetic manipulation, making human beings to order, to specification, of course whose specification and to which blueprint you're going to print them out of is one of the. . .there are all sorts of interesting possibilities in that 3rd future. There's the possibility that the government or whoever may come to control people more and more efficiently. Maybe control of emotions at a distance. It may be possible to make a person sane or insane at the flick of a switch. Biological functions may be monitored at a distance. You already have pacemakers in the heart and it's not much of a step from there to a device which would, say shut off the biological functions of the heart or the lungs of some transgressor or political malcontent. Then you get into even weirder areas where through genetic surgery and genetic manipulation we might change the entire concept of what a human being is. We may create races of new kinds of humans to specifications, sort of turn them out to somebody's blueprint. Of course the interesting question here is to whose blueprint are you going to turn people out and what are the specifications going to be. It's quite possible that in this increasingly complex 3rd future society will look nothing at all like it does now in two or three hundred years, and even human beings will be nothing like human beings are today. This is scary in a way, but a lot of this stuff is pretty grim, but at least there is some hope in that 3rd future. There is little hope at all if we all end up killing ourselves. So I don't know. Live three or four hundred years and maybe we'll find out.

Q. Okay, let's talk about your stories for a minute. A lot of your stories, especially the ones you've had in *Orbit*, have had very drab, decaying urban settings. Would you say this is the influence of living in Philadelphia?

Dozois: Well, no I can't say it's because of living in Philadelphia. Actually I've lived in much worse circumstances than South St. I lived in the lower East Side of Manhatten near 10th and Avenue A for a good many years, and probably my stories have these decaying urban atmospheres because I've existed inside decaying urban atmospheres for a good number of years. That's one point. I think another point is that many people if not the majority of people today in this country do live in decaying urban atmospheres, and it's likely that there'll be more people living in such atmospheres in the future, so certainly it seems appropriate to explore what these kind of shithouse atmospheres do to people and the kind of pressures that they put on people, and the way they shape people.

Q. Well, what do you think the future of the cities is?

Dozois: Again this depends on which of the three general futures you're going to hold as valid. In the first future they end up being destroyed in one way or another, either by atomic bomb or just general overkill of the environmental systems one way or the other. So you have masses of rubble and everybody dead etc. etc. In the 2nd future where civilization is knocked back three or four hundred years you probably have a semi-decayed situation where there would be areas still occupied and still fixed up and other areas in ruins, and adaptations to the fact that you no longer have modern technology. Probably you'd have to carry water up to the top flights of buildings that people were living in, instead of having electricity and running water, but I suspect that in that return to barbarism or at least a lower level of civilization type scenario that some of the buildings in the city would continue to be used and it would still be a population center to a certain extent, although certainly a large majority of the city would fall into ruins and be sort of shadowy battle-grounds for parties competing for survival. Now in the 3rd future any number of things could happen. It depends on how the technology advances and who's using the technology, and how rapidly the technological advances are disseminated across the population. To date they haven't been disseminated very well at all. However you realize that given sufficient technology there really isn't any reason for cities to exist anymore. They've reached the end of their term as far as social evolution is concerned. Given the right equipment there's no reason why people have to congregate together in one big huddled mass of masonry and stone and flesh. Given, say, computer terminals to deliver things to your house or print out books and, say, dependable three dimensional communications like voice and picture systems, there's no reason why. . .and an independent and reliable source of power that could be cheaply and easily manufactured, there's no reason why people couldn't be spread out over a vast area with a lot more elbow room and still be in as. . .and still have these settlements fulfill the basic purposes of having a city in the first place.

Q. Then do you think people will abandon the city or won't sheer inertia make them stick around?

Dozois: Well, like I say, again it depends. Now if you're just talking about the 3rd future, I think you'll of course get a mixture of both. What will probably happen realistically speaking is that at least at first when these advances become available the rich people will move out and have their villas in the middle of Canada or whatever, while the poor people will probably end up staying in the city out of inertia. I suspect that the cities will fall even more apart than they are at this point, and it may come to a point where they're not viable anymore even for poor people, and then depending on what kind of government you have, whether it's a humanistic government or a big brother government or a *Brave New World* pie in the sky government there'll probably be some reshuffling, at least breaking down of cities into smaller cities. Either that or we'll just have the usual shitpile mess that we end up with, and that in effect you can see all around you just by looking out your window. That depends on how pessimistic or how optimistic you're willing to be in what's going to happen in the future, whether things are going to be completely screwed up or whether they're going to proceed with any kind of order and grace. I personally doubt that there's going to be much order and grace, judging from the record of humanity for the last few thousand years. But, who knows?

Q. What kind of background do you have for being a science fiction writer? What kind do you think is needed?

Dozois: Absolutely none I would imagine, if you're talking about a scientific or technological background. I barely made it through highschool, squeeked through on the skin of my teeth on the basis of good grades in English and social studies. Flunked every math course I ever took. I even flunked typing in highschool. So, I'm hardly your renaissance man who is knowledgeable in all fields of science and technology. But I don't think you really need all that much. My basic qualification I guess is that I have read and enjoyed science fiction ever since I was a kid. In fact ever since I can remember I've been reading science fiction in one form or another, and. . .you pick up enough along the way to know at least what is generally impossible and what is generally possible. I don't think in modern SF, if ever, you need to hold a doctorate degree in nuclear engineering or physics in order to write SF. You no longer see SF stories that have pages of mathematical equations appearing as part of the narrative. I think the day of that kind of specialization is gone. What you mainly have to know as a science fiction writer is you have to have some kind of perception of what people are, which is what you need to be any kind of a writer, and added to that you have to have some kind of perception of what *things* do to people, what processes do to people, what good simple ideas do to people. What do machines do to us? What do cities do to us? What does the societal process as a whole do to us; how do we react to it? I think that's basically what you need. That type of perception is the touchstone of writing science fiction. If you don't have that kind of perception then you're just going to wind up writing adventure pap about spaceships and galactic empires, and it won't be real, it'll just be hollow. Writing for entertainment is all very well and every writer does a little bit of that, but I think you have to know what happens to people in our world today and what's likely to happen to people in the future, and indeed what has happened to people in the past before you can write any kind of a statement with any kind of validity.

Q. What writers do you think have influenced you and what writers do you admire?

Dozois: Well, there's a whole different question here between what writers have influenced you and what writers you admire. When I was a kid I ate up in ton lots writers like Edgar Rice Burroughs and A. Merritt and H. Rider Haggard, and all this glorious crew of schlockmeisters, who wrote glorious junk about far worlds with beautiful alien princesses and six-armed green monsters and people fighting it out with rayguns and swords. That's all very well, but you can't read a lot of this stuff as an adult. If you go back and try to reread ERB's Martian novels as an adult you're probably not going to make it through because they are written fairly awfully and riddled with cliches and etc. But they were influences. They led me eventually into stuff like the Heinlein juveniles and the Andre Norton juveniles, which led me eventually on to much more mature types of SF like Poul Anderson and Arthur C. Clarke and all those people, and eventually on to the stuff that I like now. As far as writers that I admire there are many writers working in SF now that I admire. I still admire Heinlein in spite of the mediocreness of his last several novels. I admire Gene Wolfe, Ursula K. Le Guin, Kate Wilhelm, James Tiptree. Any number of people that most of the readers of this newspaper have probably never heard of, which brings me to what is actually one of the biggest questions in science fiction today, which is distribution, getting the books visible to people. It's a very difficult process. We get to the point where some of the best writers in SF today are practically unknown to the general public, even to the general reading public. Even that portion of the population which still reads books for pleasure will likely not have ever heard of most of your best SF writers. Again this is because SF was so ghettoized in the pulp magazines and fell into such disrepute that it's only within the last ten years, if that long, that SF has started to come out of the shadows and get any kind of recognition. But the problem is still acute. . . SF books rarely sell in hardcover. I think the biggest bestseller in hardcover was 12,000 copies for *Stranger In A Strange Land,* though that could have been changed by now. And they rarely sell more than 100,000 copies at the very most in paperback. Now you'd have to get up to these levels to even begin to get onto the ladder of bestsellerdom as far as mainstream standards are concerned. The problem is that the organized readers of science fiction, science fiction fandom as it is known, are a relatively small group of people compared with the readership as a whole, and they're the only ones who buy SF with any systematic schedule. Most of your readers of SF are people who pick it up in the bus stand on their way to Podunk or who buy it in the train terminal or just happen to be browsing through the bookstore and hit on something with an interesting looking cover. And many of these people aren't aware that they're reading SF and don't consider themselves SF readers and the vast majority of them aren't even aware of fandom as an institution. The problem of SF is. . . I think this refers back to what you were saying earlier about whether SF has a future or not. . .is whether we can get the much larger segment of readers who read SF without thinking of themselves as science fiction readers, whether we can get them to actually seek out science fiction on a systematic basis. If we can I think that SF could be one of the biggest forms of literature of the next few years. If not, then it will remain the sort of ghettoized literature that it is. For example, how many. . . what's the circulation of this newspaper?

Q. I really don't know. 50,000 maybe.

Dozois: Well, I have a book out now in paperback from Perenial Library called *A Day In The Life.* If every reader of your newspaper or even a significant percentage of them went out and bought a copy of the book it would be a fantastic bestseller by the standards of SF. And this is only one small group of people in one portion of the country. I think that's basically the difference between the potential of the market for science fiction and the actuality of it which is piss poor to be frank. Maybe as more people come to recognize that there is such a thing as a separate genre of SF, maybe this will change.

—June 1974

Norman Spinrad

Q. What do you think is the primary value of contemporary science fiction?

Spinrad: Well, I think it's a literature of ideas. It's a literature of the infinitely possible. You can write almost anything you want. In practical terms it's the only really alive short story literature around. I think it has more value as a short fiction literature than as a novel length field. The only really good short stories with a few exceptions being written now are being written in science fiction. The so-called mainstream short story has become exhausted, and even the people who are writing that are writing a kind of science fiction.

Q. Why has it become exhausted? It held up rather nicely for a couple centuries.

Spinrad: Not really. I would say that the short story is really an early 20th century form. Again I don't profess to be a complete expert on 19th and 18th and 17th century literature, but I don't think there were very many short stories written before the 20th century. It wasn't that central to fiction. In the 19th century the novel was really central. There were a few short stories written, but I think if you look at the number of short stories written and also at the number of those stories still being read today, I think you'll find that most of them are 20th century. I guess that one of the reasons it wore down was the limited number of things to write about. Another reason is that the markets dried up. There just aren't any fiction markets. Where do you publish a non-science fiction short story. *Playboy, Oui,* and after that you're down to tacky men's magazines that want sex oriented things, or little magazines which are not too satisfying a place to base a career both in terms of money and in terms of readership, and also in terms of literary craft because it's awfully hard to get much feedback off little magazines. They're really

48

fanzines when you come right down to it.

Q. Can you give an example from your own work in which the basic idea of a short story would work as a short story but not as a novel?

Spinrad: Oh any number of them. I mean, otherwise they'd be novels. I would say almost all of them. I have never expanded a short story into a novel and probably never will. I was tempted on a thing that's come out recently called "Riding The Torch" which is probably my best piece of short fiction, 20,000 words long. People have suggested contracts and stuff but I decided that the story was 20,000 words long. "No Direction Home" I couldn't see as a novel. Somebody suggested that "Carcinoma Angels" could have been a novel. A short story is based on an idea usually, and a character or two or a situation or two. You can tell somebody what a short story is about in a few sentences. You can't tell somebody what a good novel is about in a few sentences. So the difference between the short story and the novel is in the development. You know, in the subplots, in the subsidiary characters, in subsidiary themes, in a kind of contrapuntal block type huge structure. So in a sense I suppose you could blow up any short story into a novel, but there'd have to be an awful lot more in it that wasn't in the short story. In that sense it would be a new work anyway.

Q. Which would you rather do?

Spinrad: Short stories or novels? Well, I'd rather do both. I cannot finish one novel and then start another one and start another one and just keep writing novels continuously. It would drive me completely crazy. I only did that once. I wrote *Agent of Chaos* right after finishing *The Men In The Jungle* for contractural reasons and I found out that it's an unpleasant experience. Finishing a novel is like a long bout of love-making. It's really not pleasant to have to get it up again that quickly, although it can be possible. I usually write a novel and then I don't write a novel for a year and in that period of time I would write short fiction. On the other hand I don't think I could stand writing short fiction all the time and not writing novels because it's more work and psychic effort to produce 60,000 words of short stories than to write one 60,000 novel. You have to get an idea for each story, you have to develop that idea, whereas in a novel you have one basic idea when you've got the inspiration. The hardest part for me of writing is to start something, to be inspired to write something. You need as much inspiration to write a short story as you do a novel. You have to have more inspiration to write the equivalent wordage in short stories than to write a novel. So I think writing them alternately is what I want to do.

Q. What exactly do you mean by inspiration?

Spinrad: Well, you're sitting there and you got a typewriter and you got a blank piece of paper in it and inspiration is the next step, and if that step doesn't occur you still got a typewriter and a blank piece of paper. Nothing. You know, what starts you writing a novel or a short story. That comes from somewhere, from somewhere inside, from somewhere outside, from some confluence of inside and outside factors. You say 'Hey got an idea' and then you proceed to develop the idea. But if you can't say 'Hey I got an idea' you can't develop anything. At least I can't. I guess there are some people who can. You know there are standard plots and so forth, and they say, 'All right, here's a planet with three moons or four moons' and you can ring changes on things you have already done. But for me it has to start with some idea that interests me. 'Hey, this is an idea for a story,' and then I develop that idea. Now once I have an idea the development and mental processes involved can be fairly intellectual. You know, it's something I can do by force of will. I can sit down and make myself do it even if I don't feel like it. But I have not yet found a way to make myself get an idea. If you know how I'd be very pleased if you would tell me. That's the hardest part of writing.

Q. Well, Sprague deCamp says that when he's run out of everything he opens a book at random, reads a single sentence, and shuts the book. This starts a train of thought which will develop into something.

Spinrad: Sometimes that works. Vonnegut said something which he later violated after he finished *Slaughterhouse Five*. He said, 'Well, I've written all the novels I have in me and so now I'll shut up.' And I'd like to be able to do that too. If I don't have anything to say I'd rather shut up if I can economically afford to do it, which is why I write journalism, various kinds of non-fiction. I'm writing science articles, theoretical science articles. I've been a film critic. That kind of stuff I can write between inspirations for fiction because I know I have something to write about. If I'm reviewing a movie I've seen the movie and that's what I'm writing about. If I'm writing about a scientific subject that's what I'm writing about. I wrote a piece on Chinese food for *Oui* magazine. So I knew what I was writing about—Chinese food. So I don't think I could write just fiction all the time and make a living or keep from going crazy because I can go for months at a time without getting an idea for either a short story or a novel and I can either say I'll take a vacation, depending on my bank balance which usually doesn't allow me to take a three month vacation, or I can say I'll do some non-fiction, or I can say I'm going to sit in front of this god-damned typewriter with that blank piece of paper until something comes. So I feel much better writing a broad spectrum of things. Even my fiction isn't all science fiction. I just did a novel that I wrote on for a solid year which was not science fiction. For me at any rate the more different kinds of things I'm writing the better everything flows.

Q. Was this non-science fiction novel an economic risk for you? Do you find yourself typed as a science fiction writer?

Spinrad: Well, ordinarily that's true, but this particular novel was not an economic risk. I was in New York. I was broke. I was trying to sell various science fiction novel ideas and I was having lunch with my editor—George Ernsberger at Berkeley/Putnam—and I was trying to sell him a science fiction novel idea and he said, 'No, I don't want that. I would like a big, mainstream type novel and I will pay you a large sum of money,' and I said 'Gee, that's a good idea,' and a bunch of material which had been sitting around in my head for eight years came together and I did an outline for him, and I got a contract for it before I did it. So it wasn't an economic risk. Previously, after *Bug Jack Barron*, I had just sat down and written a novel called *The Children of Hamlin* which was a mainstream novel which I still can't get published. It was serialized in the *Los Angeles Free Press* in 20 installments and was read by 200,000 people. It was bought by a publisher in England who later got out of the fiction business before they got around to publishing it. It's still never been published as a book. So that one was an economic fiasco. It was written without a contract and never sold. This one I had a contract up front on.

Q. Why didn't it sell? Could it be that something the *LA Freep* publishes and nobody else will must have scared a lot of publishers.

Spinrad: Well, it was about drugs. It drew a connection between psycho-therapy cults, drugs, and a certain famous literary agency, which I don't want to mention here if it's going to appear in print, but it's a very large literary agency and anybody who read it who knew anything about it would instantly recognize it, and most people who have read it said it was a good book—except editors who won't buy it. Even some of them said it was a good book, and add tortuous reasons why it's not commer-cial. All books are bought by women, or this is too New York oriented, or it's too this or too that. All very tortuous explanations, and I think it's a combination of being too counter-culture oriented, fears of being sued by the literary agency, stuff like that. I don't know. Maybe it's a lousey book. I don't think it's a lousey book and the circulation of the paper went up while they were serializing it, so I don't think it's without any merit at all, and a couple of other papers wanted to do second and third serializations on it. So I don't know. *Cat's Cradle* bounced twenty-four times before somebody bought it.

Q. In science fiction your best known book is probably *Bug Jack Barron*. Why do you think this made such a big splash? Was it timing?

Spinrad: Again it's hard for me to come out and say. I think it's a very good book. I think it's one of the better science fiction novels ever writ-ten, and I think it's about a subject matter which is interesting to peo-ple. You know, presidential politics, immortality, etc., and it's written in an unusual style. It has since influenced other things. I just think it was a good book and also a book that was different. It didn't so much break the taboos of the time as much as it completely ignored them. I was led to believe by my editor at Doubleday who contracted me for the book that I didn't have to worry about that stuff. Then when he saw the finished book he rejected it and it was published by somebody else. So I was not worried about taboos. I felt I could do whatever I wanted, and so I preceeded to do so. And I was also reading Marshall McLuhan at the time and that had a certain influence on me. Maybe it's because everybody watches television.

Q. This brings us to what I think is a touchy question in science fiction and that is "relevance." How far can you go being "relevant" to the time without being dated?

Spinrad: Well, I think that any fiction that is good fiction is relevant. Not necessarily to any specific time. I mean every book is set in some time period, whether it's an historical novel, a contemporary novel, or a science fiction novel. And if you're dealing with the root causes of human behavior and you're doing it in terms of the 17th century, that will have relevance to the 20th century and the 21st century and so forth. Similarly, if you're writing about the 21st century and you're writing in a psychologically real way about the characters in that setting it'll have relevance to any other period in history. I guess where you do end up being dated is a book like Fritz Leiber's *A Spectre Is Haunting Texas* which is basically a satire of Lyndon Johnson. Well, it's dead as soon as Lyndon Johnson is dead. Or Philip Roth's Nixon book. Nobody is going to be interested in that anymore. I think it's when you're doing either satire which dates with the thing you are satirizing, or a science fiction-alization thinly disguised of some present day thing.

Q. In *Bug Jack Barron* did you have contemporary things in mind, like contemporary politics, contemporary media?

Spinrad: Well, the funny thing about *Bug Jack Barron* was that it's about a situation I was anticipating in the Eighties, and except for the fact of Nixon being elected president it really all happened in the Seventies, so I was late in terms of the predictions. I felt that this sort of thing was going to go on later. I still think that the Eighties are going to be something like that, only there'll be other factors that will enter into it. No, I mean the two basic technological things in the book around which the plot completely revolves, an immortality process and the videotelephone in everybody's home, have not come to pass, so in that sense the basic core of the book was not about contemporary politics.

Q. How well do you think the book will hold up in the late Eighties?

Spinrad: Well, I'll have to see what will happen in the late Eighties. I could be completely wrong. We could have a total economic and ecological collapse. There might not be any books in the Eighties, or any people perhaps, and it won't hold up at all. We can avert that, but I think it depends on what happens in the middle Seventies, whether there will in fact be a coming together of a third party on the Left of where the Democrats are now. All the preconditions for that happening exist today. Whether the personalities to bring it together will emerge remains to be seen. I think how well it will hold up in the Eighties depends on what happens in the bulk of the Seventies.

Q. Will it hold up linguistically? I notice that the people in there are talking 1960s idiom.

Spinrad: No, I don't think they're talking 1960s idiom, but the idiom was extrapolated from the 1960s. To me anyway, most science fiction that I've read which tries to deal with a future idiom extrapolates from the 1930s. Witness Heinlein's *I Will Fear No Evil* which reads like it was written in 1920. I was trying to extrapolate from the most current possible idiom. And some of that stuff got picked up later on and became language, became idiom. So in that sense it makes itself obsolete as science fiction. As for the style of the book, that is not a conventional literary style, and there hasn't been very much written in a similar manner. The only thing I can think of is Norman Mailer's book *Why Are We In Viet Nam?* which was written at just about the same time. I couldn't have read what he was writing and he couldn't have read what I was writing. But if you read those two books you do find a curious stylistic similarity, and what he was writing wasn't exactly science fiction.

Q. What got you started writing this book?

Spinrad: I think the beginning of the book was really the whole question of immortality. Now everybody has written about immortality but nobody has written about what it would really be like because in the beginning it would have to be immortality for a few people. It would be very expensive—at least at first. And I asked what would the transition period be like? What would be the politics of such a situation? And that was the beginning and it sat in my head for a while, and then I wanted to get a character who was offered this choice, who was in the situation of being offered immortality when it was only for some kind of elite. From there I naturally got into the political ramifications of this, the whole idea of Benedict Howard's power being built on immortality. It seems to me that somebody who developed immortality would be in that kind of very strong political position, and I wanted to counterpoise that with another character who had political power based on something else. And that's where the idea of a television show came in. From there I got into how that would affect presidential politics and so forth. Starting with the immortality.

Q. Do you think that a guy like Benedict Howard, who was obviously a strong personality, and who had fought his way to the top, would snap that easily on television?

Spinrad: Well, read *The Last Days of Hitler* sometime, which I read for another book.

Q. It took the whole Russian army to undo Hitler.

Spinrad: The point is that that kind of guy is a rigid personality structure ordinarily. I was at the Hearst castle once and you stand up on the hill and you realize that William Randolph Hearst was literally the god of everything he could see from that, and when somebody who has that kind of power is challenged by somebody, I think he really can crack right down the middle. Witness Richard Nixon. The same kind of personality in some ways. But Nixon, Hitler, that kind of personality does have a tendency to split down the middle. Also in terms of the novel he was up against an expert. He was totally out of his league in terms of who was doing it to him, and I've seen things like that actually happen on television shows. I saw Paul Clasney do it to Joe Pine. I saw Joe Pine do it to a number of people. And I saw Mort Sahl go completely bananas on the air, to the point where they had to cut the show off the air and run like five minutes of dead blank air time before they figured out what the hell they were going to do. So people do occasionally go nuts on the air.

Q. Did this interest in such personalities lead you to write *The Iron Dream?*

Spinrad: Yes, there is a kind of continuity between *The Men In The Jungle, Bug Jack Barron*, and *The Iron Dream*, but *The Iron Dream* started with a conversation with Mike Moorcock about sword and sorcery and how he wrote it, and from there came the idea that there was something psychologically akin in the worst of that stuff to Nazism. And I'd always been interested in questions like, how did this happen? What the hell was Nazism? How could a thing like that happen? And somehow the whole psychological affinity between Nazism and a certain kind of sword and sorcery came to me and I said, 'Gee, if Hitler hadn't become what he did he could have easily become a sword and sorcery writer.' That was the basic impetus for the thing. But I suppose that the interest in power and how it affects the personality carried over from *Bug Jack Barron* and *The Men In The Jungle*.

Q. How did you go about writing a book which is supposed to be the product of a psychotic mind without becoming psychotic yourself?

Spinrad: By the time I finished it I think I was a little psychotic. I had been interested in the subject of Nazism for a long time, and had read the usual basic stuff like *Rise and Fall of the Third Reich* and so forth. For that book I got all the stuff that Hitler had written to get the style. I used two books really, *Mein Kampf*, and another obscure book which nobody has really heard about which he wrote about foreign policy. I read that to get his literary style and his mental style. Then I read a book called *Hitler's Dinner Conversations*. Martin Borman sat in a corner of the dining room over about a three or four year period, taking the dinner conversations down in shorthand. It's a big fat 800 page book of Hitler babbling on about every conceivable subject, and you really get more into his mind from that than from the stuff he wrote because it was coming off the top of his head. He talked about everything from making his dog a vegetarian to inventing the Volkswagen, which he did do. That's a typical crazy story. He was having dinner with Ferdinand Porsche the auto designer, and he said 'I want a car for the masses, and it should be rear-engined and air-cooled because I want it to work in Russia after we've conquered it and have all those big highways out there.' That's the way he thought, twenty steps ahead in a highly insane fashion, but we in fact have the Volkswagen, which is the last surviving thing of Nazi Germany.

54

Q. Why do you say that it requires a psychotic personality to produce sword and sorcery? It seems to me that that stuff is either serious mythic fantasy or else kind of mindless.

Spinrad: Well, of course a lot of it is written cynically. You know, Mike knows what the kinds of plots are and so forth. Yeah, a lot of it is genuine mythic fantasy, and so is Nazi Germany. In the case of Nazi Germany it was lived out. The question is really what kind of myth you're creating. I don't consider *The Lord of the Rings* a crypto-Nazi kind of thing, but a lot of this stuff is. It's the guy in the tight leather pants with the big phallic sword and a lot of bondage trips and so forth, and again it depends on the *content* of the sword and sorcery, but a lot of it is the phallic hero who ends up smashing the lower classes, the barbarians with a big weapon in a Gotterdammerung type battle, and that's a certain kind of basic sword and sorcery. I didn't say that all sword and sorcery was that way. An awful lot of it really is, though. It appeals psychologically to the same kind of thing that Hitler appealed to in the German people. You know, a kind of desire to feel powerful, to feel a mystic identity with the nation or with a large group of people, to be a superhero and so forth. Marvel Comics are the same thing, or nearly the same thing, except with characters like The Hulk which have other dimensions.

Q. Basically you've got Conan in mind, don't you?

Spinrad: Conan and the zillions of lesser things that Conan spawned, the Conan imitators.

Q. How do you account for Conan's anti-civilization attitudes? He was always his own man and never worked for anyone else. People like that don't get organized.

Spinrad: Well, Hitler was an Austrian from the outside who came into Germany, took it over, and did that. That's a superficial similarity but it's true.

Q. But somehow he got a huge, monolithic state working.

Spinrad: That's right, but it was a barbarian state. I mean like, Genghis Khan didn't have a state going; he had a horde, and really the Nazis were a horde. They didn't pay much attention to state borders after that. The army was the state. The S.S. was the state, the Gestapo was the state. It was really organized more like a barbarian horde. It had a certain territory where it came from to begin with but it's really very similar to what Genghis Khan did. There was a sort of Mongol state out there, and then it started expanding like a cancer in all directions. That's what Hitler did. I don't think that thing would have held together very long. If they'd won World War II they probably would have fallen apart within a hundred years, unless they changed radically into something else, because it was basically organized towards external conquest, towards internal order and external conquest. I think that's a kind of barbarian existence.

Q. What do you have planned now for the future?

Spinrad: Well, I have a tentative plan to write a novel about the world of science fiction if I can find a publisher crazy enough to publish it, a novel about a science fiction writer, about science fiction—

Q. Hasn't Barry Malzberg already done that?

Spinrad: *Herovit's World.* But this would not be a science fiction novel, and this would not be a humorous novel particularly, although it would have its humorous aspects. It would be a serious novel about what it's really like to be a science fiction writer in this kind of context. After all, no other kind of writers have ever been in quite this position before. It's a very complex and peculiar situation. It would cover twenty years of the history of the whole thing through the eyes of one man, not using real names but putting together composite incidents.

Q. Thank you, Mr. Spinrad.

—Lunacon, April 1975

Gordon Dickson

Q. I saw the film *Lunch With John Campbell* and I noticed that Campbell was feeding ideas to you and Mr. Harrison. How much can an editor do this? To what extent *must* any piece of writing be the writer's own inspiration?

Dickson: Let me correct you on one thing. He wasn't feeding us ideas. What he was doing, and what he was good at, and what the whole film was set up to show, was helping an author kick around an idea that was the author's idea to begin with. What John was saying was, "Let's do it this way. Do you know this interesting bit of information that might feed into it and be useful? Have you thought of doing it from this kind of angle?" If you look closely at the film you'll see that's what he was doing. Now we started out very cold on this. The background behind the film proved very interesting. As you know it was a few months before John's death. It was late in the day, and we were in downtown Manhatten. He was long overdue to go home. He wasn't feeling good. He was tired, worn out, and so on and so forth, and Harry and I had simply picked this topic for a novel about five or ten minutes before. So it was cold to all of us. There was no rehearsal; there was no planning; there was no run-through. For that matter, because of this, in the early part of the film, you'll see that we're a long ways apart, John and Harry and I. Later on we begin to zero in and get together on the thing. This of course, for the teaching purposes of the film, is the main point—to show experienced professionals zeroing in on a story idea.

Q. Do you find this kind of prior discussion to always be helpful? For example, some writers say that if they talk at all about a story yet unwritten they'll never write it.

Dickson: There are basically two categories of writers. The unconscious writer would rather not talk about what he's doing. This is because he's afraid that if he talks about it he will destroy the mental process which is fermenting at the present time. Then there's the conscious writer who not only can talk about his writing but likes to talk about it. Instead of destroying it, the more he discusses it the stronger it gets. What the conscious writer is, which is the type I belong to, Ben Bova belongs to, Harry belongs to, John Campbell belonged to, is somebody who is thinking up new things all the time, testing them against the idea in the back of his head, and rejecting what won't work and accepting what will. By and large the more experience the writer has the more he is likely to be a conscious writer.

Q. Do you find this varies between writers who are idea-oriented and writers who are not?

Dickson: No, it seems to cover the whole spectrum. I can go down the list of our names in science fiction, and our proportion of conscious writers is very heavy compared to mainstream, where the proportion is overwhelmingly unconscious, people who don't want to talk about it. Part of it is the same research syndrome you probably heard me talking about down on the panel, the fact that you have a bunch of writers who are interested not only in writing but in a number of other fields to the point where they are close to being semi-professional in most of these areas. It's surprising. Bob Silverberg, although he has no degree in archeology, for example, could go on an archeological dig in Egypt tomorrow and be an entirely useful member of the expedition. The same way with a lot of others. Harry Harrison, for example, to pull another name out of the woodwork, the man who collaborated with me on *Lifeboat* and was in this film you were talking about, was a professional artist, an illustrator, before he was a writer. He also was a writer of medical articles, which means that he knows a good share of what a good medical technician knows, and a fair share of what a good number of M.D.s know. This is again a characteristic of the field, a characteristic of the people who write it. Now you can't generalize from science fiction writers to writers in general because we are kind of a breed apart.

Q. What field outside of writing do you know best?

Dickson: I know a number of fields, mainly because I've gone into them on a hobby basis, or a writing basis. The one that comes most quickly to mind is the fact that I know the 14th century, England and Europe, pretty doggone well, because the first novel of the Childe cycle is about Sir John Hawkwood, who has been called the first of the modern generals, and was one of the great early condottieries. His picture still hangs in the Duomo, the cathedral in Florence. He was captain-general of Florence in his eighties. As a matter of fact my thesis in Childe is that he's the man who, with inferior forces stopped Giangalleazo Visconti from taking over all of Italy and changing the whole situation of the Renaissance and consequently all of history since.

Q. I have heard about your plans for putting historical and contemporary novels into the Childe series. Do you think you'll run into trouble publishing this as a series because you have been typed as a science fiction writer?

Dickson: At one time I think I would have, but both I and the science fiction field have changed in the last 26 years that I've been writing and by the time I get around to doing the historicals and the contemporaries, which are to be done as separate books in any case, and I have the whole twelve books put together in one area, the problem won't be that I'm labelled a science fiction writer. For one thing by that time I won't be known only as a science fiction writer, since I will have done historicals and contemporaries most recently. A lot of people who will have read them won't know about my science fiction.

Q. Do you think you can get one publisher to publish the whole thing as a series, despite the fact it runs over category lines?

Dickson: Eventually I don't think there'll be any problem. I think if I had the historicals and contemporaries done I could almost do it nowadays, I mean in this year of 1975, if I had all the work done. I have yet to write a book in the Childe cycle or outside it that hasn't paid its way, in other words one that the publisher hasn't made a profit out of. Now by the time I have the whole series done all twelve books will have proved their profit-making abilities. So it isn't too hard to find a publisher to do it all at once.

Q. Have you written any of the non-science fiction in the series?

Dickson: No. I've done nothing but the science fiction for two reasons. One is that I haven't had the time to do all the necessary research for the historicals and I haven't had the peace of mind to do the contemporaries. Secondly, simply because I was wound up in the science fiction area. I'm just now getting to the point where I can afford to contemplate the expenditure of both time and money that's involved in doing any one of these other novels. It would be a full year, which means what it costs me to live for a year plus, for example in the case of Hawkwood, travel. I'll have to go to Italy for about three months. In other words, they're expensive projects. But I'm getting to the point where I can afford them.

Q. Then it will not be an economic risk to do so?

Dickson: It will be an economic risk, but the point is it will be an economic risk I can stand to take the chance on. I literally couldn't afford to do this earlier. I couldn't afford to take a year off from writing science fiction and do a historical novel. I didn't want to do it improperly.

Q. Did you have the plan for the whole series worked out ahead of time, or did it just sort of grow?

Dickson: It's very interesting. I was up at the Milford Science Fiction Conference when it happened. I lay awake most of one night and the next day I spent about three hours talking it out with Richard McKenna, Mac who wrote *The Sand Pebbles,* and Mac acted more like an ear than anything else. He just sat there and listened while I worked it out. In the process of talking it out I took these vague shapes and put them into words, and the pattern hasn't varied at all from that initial conception. I haven't even added to it. Now one thing that has developed is a lot of short stories that I'd like to do, simply because a lot of interesting characters have cropped up, in the science fiction end particularly, that I may get around to writing. But they aren't necessary to the Cycle. I speak of them as being peripheral to the Cycle. They're entertainments. The Cycle itself makes a thematic argument.

Q. Couldn't you just have a thirteenth volume of related short stories?

Dickson: It wouldn't be a thirteenth volume. It would simple be short stories tied in with the Cycle. The Cycle is specifically what I describe as a Cycle, three historicals, three contemporaries, six science fiction novels. This states the whole argument. Just for the fun of it, having built this particular castle, it's nice to go out and build a few outbuildings too.

Q. Since the whole series has not been written, and since we've only seen the science fiction parts of it, could you tell me what the overall argument is?

Dickson: The overall thematic argument of the Childe cycle is that man started an evolutionary move at about the 14th century, the time of the Renaissance, and we have halfway accomplished it at this present time in the 20th century. In about five hundred years from now we will have accomplished it completely. It is neither a physical nor a mental evolution, but an ethical evolution. And it's accomplished through what I call either the Alternate universe or the Creative universe. Its end result will be what I tab "the responsible man." The responsible man is somebody who has all the powers in the world. He has the powers of a god, in fact, but he doesn't misuse them any more than a sane man would cut his throat with his razor while he's shaving in the morning.

Q. What makes you think such a man will ever come about? Humanity's history so far hasn't had a very good batting average.

Dickson: No, as a matter of fact I disagree with you. I think we're halfway there right now. If you study the 14th century, if you study the Middle Ages, you discover that empathy was almost non-existent. Sympathy was there, but empathy was almost non-existent. Nowadays we have people, particularly in the Western world, particularly in this country, who feel a duty to have a conscious response to the mistreatment of animals, children, and other people as far as they will under certain social situations. We may not always treat them well, but we feel guilty when we don't. Now that's a long step forward from the Middle Ages. The character in the 14th century who attracted me first, long before the Cycle—I was going to do a historical novel called *The Pikeman*—was a young Swiss member of a Cantonal levy. Swiss cantons used to hire their young men out as cannon-fodder during the Renaissance, as pikemen. This is very interesting because the pikemen eventually stopped the mounted horsemen. The mailed horseman was supreme until the pikeman came along. This is not because men weren't willing to run up against these pikes, but horses weren't. Horses would get close to the pikes and go crazy. They're not going to go up there and get themselves stuck. Once they got close they wanted to get away. So it ruined a charge, because a man in full armor on horseback relied on the fact that the point of his lance hit you with about three tons of weight behind it. This is what made him irresistable. But it didn't do any good if his horse would slow down to a walk and then start backing up. All right, the point is that these pikemen—I've forgotten the names for them, marvellous German names, but essentially the first line means "Lots of luck, Charlie" and the next one is "Well you've got a chance," and the third one is "Well, these twenty-year men are all the lucky ones." This is literally what they translate out to. Now the point is that this Swiss pikeman was to see a particular Renaissance type, and this was a Renaissance noble who was intellectually quite a match for a well-educated, aesthetically-minded modern man, except for one area, and that's the human area. He would listen to and admire good music. He would read literature and talk about it critically, calmly, sensibly, intellectually. He would admire good paintings, and art. Then he could walk out of the house he had been having these discussions in and he would enjoy setting his dogs on a beggar just for the fun of seeing the beggar torn to bits. In other words he had what we in the modern terms think of as a tremendous split in his attitude. We don't think of somebody who is artistically responsive, as being a whole person if at the same time they are humanly completely unresponsive. We tend to think that these things have to go together. They don't necessarily. Medieval man didn't see any disparity in this at all. This is because medieval man made a strong distinction between the actual and the ideal. Now during the Middle Ages, if you were a land owner and pretty well off—you might have even had your own captive priest. Let's say you're in the middle of France somewhere. Because you have your own priest you build your own chapel and you hold Mass and you invite the neighbors in. They don't have one. So here's Sunday and the neighbors have dropped over—they're all gentle people, respectable upper class. They come in and they sit in the church. Now your priest gets up and will celebrate Mass, and also preaches a sermon. This priest, except on Sunday, has been treated like a sort of second-class servant. Nobody does him any favors. He's sent to literally hew wood and fetch water, and things like that. He's got a little bit of respectability but actually he's made fun of by the knights, and things like this. And Sunday he gets it all back. He gets a chance to lecture them all. I have seen copies of sermons given by these priests, and they are very much like a modern revivalist sermon. One of them in particular that comes to mind right now is literally, "You lords in your castles, you proud men. You think you're much better than Piers Plowman out here, who plows the earth. But what are you? You do no good, you bring forth no fruit. He brings forth fruit. He is a noble man. You are the dregs, etc." They would sit there, these men who are used to chopping people apart, and they would cry great tears, and say "Oh it's true, I'm no good." They'd go out of the chapel and say, "Boy that was a real good sermon," and outside the door they'd run into their own Piers Plowman, and they'd kick him out of the way. He had nothing to do with the man the priest was talking about. The priest was talking about the idealized plowman. Now, this is why the Renaissance man, the Renaissance intellectual, can have a split nature. We are half way there. We don't believe in this bit. That is why I want to do the historical. By doing it I would be drawing a portrait of what we *now* consider a semi-psychotic person, who was not considered so in terms of his own social order and time. Now we go one step further, and what I argue and presuppose in the Childe cycle is that five hundred years from now a 20th century man with his failings in empathy would be considered a semi-psychotic individual.

Q. Specifically, what kind of 20th century characteristics do you have in mind?

Dickson: The kind of thing you see in the newspapers. We profess kindness and we profess concern for our fellow man, and so forth, but we don't act it. We find excuses not to. We find ourselves caught in a sort of historical machinery which is not really our fault since we inherited it, in which it is very hard to live the ideal life that we profess. So sometimes we do and sometimes we don't. The man I'm talking about five hundred years from now would have evolved the machinery to live the life he professed.

Q. When you're talking about evolution, do you mean that this kind of ethical improvement has survival value?

Dickson: Yes. It actually has survival value in our present time. If you consider men in the Western world right now you discover that within the confines of our own particular social gestalt this kind of ethic response does have survival value. It works in this way: If you demonstrate it you will develop a community of people around you who like you and respond to you. These will act as a cushion and an assistance in the periods which would otherwise be difficult. Now it takes time to do this. You can't do it overnight. But over a twenty-year period or something like that, socially this kind of ethical response pays off even in our own time.

Q. But how well does it pay off in competition with the people who don't have it?

Dickson: Well, it doesn't seem to pay off at all on the short range. In the long range it does. It's very interesting. I'm now 51. To look back on old friends of mine who did not show this type of ethical response and who are still alive now and making a good living, I see that their lives are in comparison with the life I lead very barren, cold, and lonely. I really lead a very happy life. Now, accident has an awful lot to do with it. It just happens that science fiction, which used to be something that everybody giggled about, has turned out to be something fairly respectable, and it has developed by accident and by the situations of the field into a condition in which most of the in-group are like a small, warm community. Now this doesn't always happen. It has happened, however. And the only reason it has happened is that by a curious freak of the field and the people involved, most of the professionals in these areas, not only the writers but everybody involved, the writers, the artists and so forth, are themselves very bright and very warm people. But to live together in this type of environment they have to be empathic, they have to be other-responsive. And of course they are. In essence we're getting this little in-community, and this is exactly the kind of community I'm pointing towards in the Childe cycle.

Q. One problem in this warm community of science fiction fandom is that it tends to become very conservative, resistant to change.

Dickson: For example?

Q. Well, you might recall something called "The New Wave" which they made a lot of noise about a few years ago. I think this showed more than anything else that the science fiction audience is extremely conservative, and will react adversely to anything they haven't read *before*. If all humanity became like that, wouldn't this tend to slow down progress?

Dickson: Your assumption that this community is conservative is one I don't agree with. And it's founded on another assumption, and that is that the "New Wave" existed, which it didn't. There are periods of experimentation in literature, which happen regularly. This particular wave of experimentation that came along within the past six years was simply the last of a series of waves of experimentation in the science fiction field. We renew literally about twice a decade. I think I mentioned in my guest of honor speech yesterday that there are a bunch of new writers coming along who are entirely different from the ones that came along five years before, ten years before, fifteen years before that. However these aren't being tagged as precedent breakers. The label "New Wave" isn't being used, but it could be very well. Again they're as different from the people before as the others were. There's this continual influx of new blood, new push. This is what makes the field an interesting one to work in. And simply because the front stage is being continually usurped every five years by a new wave of writers that weren't around, it can't become conservative.

—Disclave, 1975

Ben Bova

Q. You are now editing the country's leading science fiction magazine. How did you get the job?

Bova: Very easily. I was asked if I wanted to be considered and I said, "Yes," and about two months later I was called up by the management of Conde Nast and they said, "Would you care to come down to New York for an interview?" and I did and we talked for a while and they decided they'd like to have me be the editor.

Q. What are you doing as editor now? Are you trying to keep the magazine as it was, or change it?

Bova: Well, there are several things I'm trying to do. One is I'm trying to have fun, which is easy to do. The second is I'm trying to make sure that *Analog's* readers are entertained with each issue, and hopefully if they're entertained enough they'll tell their friends about it and we'll get more readers.

Q. What do you think of the policies of your predecessor? Are you following them?

Bova: I think that the major part of Campbell's policy was to give the *Analog* audience a battleground for ideas, an arena for different kinds of ideas. And all I'm trying to do is follow that policy and make the ideas as varied as can be and to bring them in from as many points of the compass as possible, so that each issue will have things in it that a large number of our readers will get upset about. When we stop getting them upset, then we've started boring them and the magazine will flop.

Q. You mean you deliberately create controversies?

64

Bova: Not necessarily a controversy, but we try and present stories which have strong idea content. For example, when we did Fred Pohl's story "The Gold At The Starbow's End" an awful lot of *Analog* readers got very upset about that for a number of reasons. Some of them considered it to be out and out fantasy rather than science fiction. Many of them got upset with the references to sex. Most of them felt it was rather far out on the left side of the political spectrum and many of our readers didn't like that. On the other hand, as I've tried to point out to some critics, any kind of story which is strong enough to make someone write an angry letter, that's a story that hit that person and hit him hard. A few issues later we ran a story called "Generation Gaps" in which the left wing, anti-science types, the kinds of people who used to be called hippies, were pretty roundly castigated, and we had an uproar from the *left* side of our audience saying "Obviously this proves that *Analog* is still a fascist magazine and unworthy of our attention." Yet these people keep buying the magazine and keep reading it.

Q. Do you think it is the function of a science fiction magazine to do political satire on current events?

Bova: I think SF is a field of literature that is ideally suited to do political satire, and it has been doing so since at least Swift's time, and probably if you go back to Aristophanes you can make some connections between the fantasies he wrote and the political situation of the day. *Lysistrata* is not really science fiction, but it is using an unreal situation to parody a real one.

Q. Do you think that a simple caricature of "hippies" makes a good science fiction story?

Bova: Yes. It isn't all that simple anyway. I think what makes a good SF story is taking a situation or an idea and carrying it as far as you can carry it and seeing what happens. It's sort of like the old engineering idea of testing to destruction. And if you have a group of people who believe that science is inherently evil, that technology is inherently bad, and everybody in command of society believes this way, you're going to have a society that is unable to fold its own diapers, and this is what the writer said in "Generation Gaps."

Q. Is this legitimate extrapolation?

Bova: Sure. It's as legitimate as extrapolating the current political situation into 1984.

Q. Do you think that the kind of reactions you get from the readers reflects well on them and on the magazine? Like the letters you've had from some people complaining about the sexual content of *Analog* stories only shows that they've never read any literature at all hardly. They would probably get upset about D. H. Lawrence and such things which are now very passe.

Bova: No, I think they've got a perfect right to be upset about the things that upset them. And remember that what we are publishing are a few letters from people who have a strong opinion. What we don't publish are the hundreds of letters coming back saying, "These guys are idiots and the story is perfectly fine." It's much more interesting for me to publish letters that attack what we're doing than to publish the letters that simply pat us on the back. I think everybody would get pretty bored with a Brass Tacks column that is filled with nothing but congratulations. Letters that have a specific point of view, that attack something, that complain about something, or that have an interesting point to make are the kinds of letters that I find profitable to run. Some of the others I answer personally, but many of them are too congratulatory to run. It would look like I'm writing them myself.

Q. Doesn't it disturb you that some of the controversies, such as the one over the sex in Haldeman's "Hero," are carried on by what seem to be the most literarily backward people who are still reading at all?

Bova: I don't know what you mean by literarily backward. These are people who read, who enjoy what they're reading, who get upset enough to send a letter—they've got enough literary abilities to compose a letter and express their views. Compared to most Americans this is lightyears ahead of the literary talents or ambitions of most people. We have become a nation of television watchers. Do you realize that when a science fiction book is published in England it sells as many copies as it does in the U.S.? So how many English adults are there? It's a nation of about 50 million, compared to our 200 million, yet their reading population is just as strong as ours.

Q. What do you think about improving the literary sophistication of *Analog* and SF in general?

Bova: Well, as far as *Analog* is concerned we are trying to stretch our readership's imagination from time to time, bringing in stories that don't exactly fit in the cast-iron *Analog* mold. I think this is something that Campbell constantly did, that when you thought you had him figured out, when you knew exactly what kind of stories Campbell liked and would buy, he went out and did something different, and changed and pulled the rug out from under you. What we're trying to do is bring the readership along to recognize stories that are not quite engineer-meets-problem, engineer-solves-problem, and at the same time I think this will bring more readers and more writers into the *Analog* fold.

Q. Certainly in the last few years of the Campbell editorship *Analog* was sort of getting off into a corner by itself. It didn't seem to have much to do with the field at all.

Bova: Well, you're mistaking the tail and the dog. *Analog* had at that time 110,000 readers. It's gone up something from then. SF fandom had several thousand people. Campbell's audience was much bigger, much more intellectual than SF fandom. John was not editing his magazine for SF fans; he was publishing for his audience.

Q. I would point out that a writer like Roger Zelazny rose to enormous prominence without ever having appeared in *Analog* and there is a long list of other writers like that. It doesn't seem that *Analog* was overlapping with the other magazines, or with book publishing very much.

Bova: Why should it?

Q. You would get a wider readership I would think.

Bova: No. Every science fiction fan reads *Analog* anyway. I think the people who don't are in a small minority, and if every SF fan did read *Analog* it would be less than a tenth of the total readership of the magazine. So you take all the people who were at the world convention—how many were there? 4500? Well, we have 150,000 readers every month. Buyers. God knows how many readers, because we estimate that three to five people read each issue bought, so what difference does it make? No, I personally am an SF fan myself and I like fandom, and I think it makes an important contribution to the world and to *Analog* magazine, and it is true that Campbell went his own way and built up his own readership, but I don't think Campbell really depended on SF fandom per se for the success of his magazine. And I can't either. I think it's marvellous that the fans are coming back to *Analog*, the ones who had been turned off by Campbell's policies, but I don't think that's a very large number of people. I mean though many fans complained loudly about Campbell they read him every month because even when you disagreed with John, which was always, he was interesting, he was provocative. He forced you to examine your own preconceptions and defend you own ideas. And the day that fandom or any other group of people came to Campbell and said "We agree with you," he would change the subject and go off on another argument. John's *forte* was picking fights.

Q. That's what he did with his editorials, but the fiction in the magazine itself was another matter. Do you think the *Analog* readership reads for the editorials or for the fiction?

Bova: I think they read for both. Certainly I don't think that the editorials that I write are anywhere near the quality and provocativeness of John's. I think our views on the world are very different, and we have totally different points of view, but I think John was a real genius in writing essays, essays that could take a common wisdom and shake it until the bones fell out. As far as the fiction that John published, that's what he published and that's what his readers read. We're publishing many of the same writers, but we're also publishing other people who either had not or would not work for John. Now a lot of John's writers, a lot of people who wrote with prominence for John, are just not sending stories in to *Analog* now, and I think it's because many of them have just stopped writing SF. For example I haven't seen anything from Christopher Anvil or Eric Frank Russell. We haven't been able to publish anything from Mack Reynolds for example. Several other writers, who are very well liked, constantly asked for by the readers, but who have just not sent in stories. On the other hand we have Roger Zelazny. We published a short story of his, and we will have a novel of his coming out in the spring. [1975] I've just bought a novelet that he did, and lots of other writers who are either newcomers to science fiction or newcomers to *Analog* are popping into the magazine quite regularly.

Q. The trademark of *Analog* all along has been the hard science and technology story. What do you think is the appeal of this?

Bova: I think largely the same appeal that science itself has. The typical *Analog* reader I think firmly believes that if you use your human intelligence you can conquer almost anything, that man is the measure of all things. People tend to think there is a dichotomy between science and the humanities and yet science is the most humanistic pursuit man has ever invented, and science fiction, especially the hard science fiction that *Analog* has specialized in, is a very optimistic, hopeful kind of literature in which there is a sort of bias towards human intelligence being able to meet and master any challenge that is hurled at it. Now not every story works that way, and sometimes the hero loses. But he always tries. There is no story in *Analog* in which the hero just sits on his haunches and says "Woe is me. I can't understand it," or "I can't cope with it," and just sort of sticks his finger in his nose and rolls over and dies.

Q. What areas of the sciences do you think are most promising for speculation and writing science fiction?

Bova: Genetics undoubtedly. The physicists have been the blue sky people for a long time, probably since Galileo, but now biophysics, the biomolecular studies, genetics and biochemistry are really the exciting areas. We have within our conceptual grasp at least the ability to create a physically perfect race, a race in which there are no genetic defects at all, and every human being is as physically strong and healthy and as perfect as can be imagined. And this also presents grave problems and dangers, because where we can manipulate people genetically, essentially tailor-make the next generation, a Hitler or a Stalin for example might want a generation of slaves to serve him.

Q. Wouldn't a genetically perfect race be immune to most or all diseases and have an indefinite lifespan?

Bova: I don't know about the indefinite lifespan because nobody knows what really causes ageing, but it would be immune to genetic defects, genetic diseases. I think that human beings would still be susceptible to bacteria and viruses. But hopefully if we know that much about genetics we'll know how to really do medicine. I have a feeling that what we know of medicine today is different from what was known in the Middle Ages mainly because of advances in surgery and techniques for making sharper surgical instruments. To my mind surgery is an admission that you don't understand medicine. Hopefully if we really understand genetics people won't have to get cut up to have the evil parts of them excised. We'll be able to do it right.

Q. I've heard biologists claim that there is a lifespan built into the genetic code for all species. Now if this were erased, wouldn't you have a very long lived race?

Bova: I don't know. I think that point of view is a supposition. I don't think anybody can really say definitely what causes ageing, what causes the final death due to old age, whether it is a genetic problem, whether it is glandular, whether it's just sheer boredom. I haven't the faintest idea and I don't think anyone else does either. But certainly if knowledge extends we may be able to figure out why and postpone it, or at the very least use mechanical or even biological aids to indefinitely prolong human life. For example, as you get older your arteries harden and eventually your heart gives out. Today it is possible to produce plastic pumps that will help the heart along. If we really knew something about genetics we would have the body create a new heart for itself. After all, your body built a heart once. The information is still there, but we just don't know how to tease it into building a new heart. But conceptually, I don't see any reason why it couldn't be done.

Q. The type of writing you are editing believes that man can solve just about anything, but do you think there are limits to human knowledge? Are there things we cannot know?

Bova: Have you ever read *As On A Darkling Plain*?

Q. No.

Bova: Well, I will not answer that. You go read it.

Q. Well, I had in mind something like Lem's *Solaris* in which he puts scientists up against something which cannot be understood.

Bova: I don't think any writer can write something which cannot be understood.

Q. He sort of faked it.

Bova: Yes, I'm well aware of the way writers fake things. I've done it myself. But really, read *As On A Darkling Plain* because there in 60,000 well-chosen words I answered your question.

Q. What areas of speculation do you think are producing the best SF now?

Bova: That's a little difficult to answer because the stories come from all points of the compass. One of the things that struck me in a story from Alex and Phyllis Eisenstein called "The Weather on Mars" which was in our December issue which was devoted to stories about Mars.

They point out in this story that once you have the ability to cryogenically suspend people, to put them to sleep at very low temperatures so that they can be kept indefinitely in suspended animation, you have given the human race the capacity to engage in enormously long projects. The same people can begin a project in the 20th century and carry it out over ten centuries, a hundred, whatever you like. Wake up one month out of the year every hundred years, see how the project is going, give orders, change things if necessary, then be frozen again. Now all the undertakings that we've ever been involved in, with the exception of a very few, have been one generation jobs. Human beings don't like to start projects that they know they will never see the end of. If we can successfully freeze people cryogenically so that we can make their lifespans indeterminately long, there is no end to the timespan of the projects that we could undertake. Star flight will be probably the one that comes to mind most easily, but there are others just as well. How about a program to prevent a new ice age? It would take geological timespans to put into effect, and might be a lot of fun to do. I'd like to see a story about somebody who figures out that the sun is going nova, and can predict it well enough so that they know when, and a project is undertaken to stop it. Just for sentimental reasons. I'm sure that by that time the human race will be spread around large parts of the galaxy, but just because it is our pleasure and because Earth is our original home, our people return and try to prevent the sun from going nova. That might be an interesting story.

—Sept. 1974

Ted White

Q. What is your biggest problem as editor of *Amazing* and *Fantastic?*

White: Money. Lack thereof.

Q. As simple as that?

White: Well, you can carry that in as many directions as you like. You can follow the ramifications of lack of money through low editorial budgets, low production budgets, lack of promotion. Every single direction in which the magazines seem to fall short can usually be traced back to a lack of money.

Q. Is this true in a magazine as specialized as *Fantastic?* With its sword and sorcery emphasis it has no competitors. It is the *only* market for fiction of this type in short lengths.

White: Well, that's true, but on the other hand it's not making much money. [laughs] Its sales in general are lower than *Amazing's.* Its distribution seems even more limited than *Amazing's.* If I see one of the two magazines on sale somewhere and not the other it's always *Amazing,* and not *Fantastic.* It seems to me that with adequate promotion and so forth we could get enough copies of *Fantastic* out that we would be selling sixty, eighty, a hundred thousand copies of each issue. I feel the audience is there.

Q. Is it an audience for just Conan-type sword and sorcery, or for general fantasy? For example, could you go more in the direction of *Unknown?*

White: Well, that's hard to say. I view *Unknown* as a kind of a fantasy magazine. It had a very particular Campbellian approach to fantasy involved in it. Generally speaking this boiled down to no matter how fantastic your premise, your followup should be logical. Therefore you found little surrealism. You found no Victorian fantasy to speak of. You didn't find a very wide spectrum of fantasy in *Unknown*. Even though *Unknown* seemed to cover different types of fantasy from heroic adventure to consequences of magic sort of things, I think *Fantastic* has a much broader spectrum than *Unknown*. It tries to include the kind of stories that *Unknown* published, but it doesn't stop there. It is a more experimental magazine, a more radical magazine. It is far wider ranging. I'd have to say that if I wanted to publish a magazine that was mostly like *Unknown* I'd have a hard time finding enough material to fill an issue. The closest thing to it was Sprague de Camp's novel, *The Fallible Fiend*.

Q. Some fantasy is selling very well these days. *Lord of the Rings* continues to sell, and even William Morris' *The Well At The World's End* has gone through something like four printings.

White: Well, look at *Watership Down*, which is fantasy on the level that *Bambi* is fantasy at the very least. It seems to have overtones of higher levels of fantasy. It's Tolkien-like in many respects. The rabbits are quite hobbit-like. You have a book like that on the best seller list.

Q. Can *Fantastic* tap into that kind of a market?

White: To the readership of that? I think it's a mistake to think that a magazine can tap into the readership market of a particular book. *Coven 13* was founded on the notion that you could tap into the sales of *Rosemary's Baby*. And they were wrong. They were just flat wrong. These things are ephemeral. That's like people trying to cash in on James Bond, and James Bond was a bigger fad than most. No one has successfully exploited Tolkien, and Tolkien represents a fairly durable "fad." From the early sixties to the present Tolkien continues to be immensely popular. I think people are looking for stuff on that level, but stuff on that level is not produced on a monthly basis for a magazine. It takes a man's lifetime.

Q. Then doesn't it follow that there is a sort of weakening of the tea, so to speak, when a writer writes magazine fiction? Can a masterpiece be produced this way?

White: No, I didn't say that, but very few people produce very many masterpieces. Let's say the person is Tolkien. He spends twenty or thirty years working on it. He hones it, he crafts it. It's the work of a lifetime. He has no sense of immediacy and deadlines. He's content to let another year pass while he works out a few details. He's more likely just from his working habits to arrive at something permanent. But the average writer who writes stuff on a fairly frequent basis has to get the wordage out, keep his material in circulation, keep getting those sales and those checks coming in, because of course what you write now may bring money in six months to a year from now, and you have to have done something six months to a year ago to bring in money now. You're constantly doing something, and you may produce a masterpiece too, but if you do so it's more likely to be either accidental or something you can take a long time working up to in the process of doing a lot of lesser stuff. Either way your masterpiece is going to exist in addition to a lot of other stuff which is no masterpiece, some of which may be nowhere even close to it. All that stuff is going to be in print for people to look at, if it was publishable in the first place. That's what the magazine is. The magazine is where all that stuff appears.

Q. There are many writers—Michael Moorcock is a good example—who, if they took three years rather than three weeks on a book, could be very, very good. Isn't this need for money actually damaging the field?

White: Well, you could take the point of view that the field has a sort of Sturgeon's Law applying to it, that 90% of whatever appears is going to be dreck. The other ten percent is going to have a few genuine masterpieces in it, and you just take those masterpieces with the other 90%. I don't think the field is either harmed or helped by this. You always have a certain number of people who are gentleman amateurs at whatever endeavor they're involved in, and you've got other people who are, to put the word in its best sense,'hacks, people who are expected to turn out something that never falls below a minimum level of competency, and sometimes, perhaps often, rises above it. Somebody like Poul Anderson, for instance. You *know* that Poul Anderson is never going to be less than entertaining. You start with that, and then you consider that a certain amount of Poul Anderson stories are either going to win an award that year or be in contention for one. There was a time when those would be, perhaps, ten to twenty percent of the total wordage he would have published in a single given year. No, I think the percentage is higher because he's publishing less. Take someone like Keith Laumer. Keith Laumer has written a couple of really good stories. Keith Laumer has written a *lot* of really entertaining books. You can easily forget just how difficult it is for Keith to do what he does. I have tried writing Keith Laumer type fiction, and stuff that he makes look effortless, transitions from one point of view to another, from one character to another, from one scene to another—if you stop and analyse it you may think there is no connection, and you may ask yourself as a writer "How can I bridge that gap?" Keith just moves right across. He keeps you moving. He has a tremendous talent for picking up the reader by the scruff of the neck and dragging him into the story, never letting him go long enough to figure out whether the story makes sense or not. That's not easily done. Moorcock, whom you mentioned earlier, is somebody who has openly made no bones about the fact that he hacked for a living. He wrote dialogue in comic book balloons for his first job, when he was still a kid, for a thing called *Tarzan Adventures.* He has ground out a wide variety of what would be called pulp fiction just to stay alive, and at the same time has entertained high ambitions. I would say that he's a most unusual case and not typical at all. Very few writers try to operate on as many different levels of ambition as he does. I mean usually they're all Brian Aldisses or they're all Vargo Stattens. [laughs]

73

Q. Getting back to editing, what do you do besides select the stories you want?

White: Well, these are all individual and unique situations, and anything I tell you about my job would tell you nothing about what Jim Baen does or Ed Ferman does or what Ben Bova does. Every one of us has a wholly different setup, although I would suppose mine is closest to Ed Ferman's, in that for the most part two people do most of the work of putting out *Amazing* and *Fantastic*, namely Sol Cohen and myself. Both operate out of our houses. Well, I pick up manuscripts at the post office; I take them to a weekly writer's group meeting. These people take the manuscripts they think they can handle, and in turn hand over anything they picked up the week before that they think I should read. Periodically they get themselves replenished with rejection slips. The manuscript then moves on to my desk where it joins some others, which I read in binges and then grow sick of for a period of time until they pile up and I have to read more. I've read manuscripts just too long. I'm reaching a point where it's very hard for me to look at them with any pleasure. It surprises me when I pick something up that really involves me, and makes me forget that I'm reading a manuscript.

Q. To what extent do you have to choose stories that the readers will like, and which will sell copies, as opposed to stories that you personally like?

White: Well, I don't do that much at all in *Amazing*. I would suppose to some extent the ranker sword and sorcery I've published in *Fantastic* would fall into that classification. But I don't know that I could say I am cynically buying stories that I thnk my readers will like more than I do. I've discovered that it doesn't really matter what you put in a magazine, as long as it's readable. Someone will like it and someone will hate it. I can publish an issue where I thought every story was really brilliant, it was a dynamite issue, and I may get mostly letters of complaint about the stories in that issue. I may put together an issue that I regard as pretty off material that I just had to get out of the inventory, and I'll get letters from readers saying, "Jesus that's a great story. They don't write 'em like that anymore." It doesn't matter what you do on that level. You can't edit for your readers. That's a fallacy. Your readers follow. They don't direct you. You have to edit for your own tastes. But you never edit exclusively for your own tastes. There are too many other expediencies, contingencies, and problems that arise. It may become politic to take a story that you don't like a whole lot in order to get a story that you think you will like. You may decide that a particular writer, whose stuff you want, is worth taking lesser stuff from so you can get some better later on. In my case every so often my publisher sends me a copy of a manuscript and informs me that he's already purchased it unread or with the opinion of the New York fan who reads manuscripts for him.

Q. This is presumably something from a big name, right?

74

White: In some cases but not always. Sometimes it will be somebody who has some personal ties with the publisher. His son wrote something and gives it to the publisher and the publisher gives it to me, and he says, "If this isn't absolutely dreadful, you should publish it." I'm not going to tell you which stories those are. Sometimes they're fairly obvious. [laughs] So, you know, that intrudes. Then there is the awareness that if we publish a Conan story the issue tends to sell five to ten thousand copies more, and you can bet I'm not about to reject a Conan story.

Q. You say the readers follow, they don't lead—

White: There are a few exceptions. Conan is one of the exceptions.

Q. Well, there have been a lot of magazines where the readers have just stopped following. The very late *New Worlds* is the best example I can think of.

White: Well, eccentricity carried to excess will certainly turn off all but a very small, devoted coterie of readers. You have to make up your mind whether you're going for a small, devoted coterie or whether you're going for a broader audience. Certainly from the point of view of keeping the magazines commercially viable we have to think in terms of broad audiences. That's why I try to put a lot of different things into *Fantastic*, so that there is something there for almost everyone, and hopefully enough so that the person will want to buy the next issue, because a magazine, you know, sells any given issue on the basis of what the reader already encountered in the magazine previously. If a reader has been turned off by the last issue, he is very unlikely to pick up the next. And that works in reverse. You do a really dynamite issue and sometimes you pick up a wave of sales.

Q. How many manuscripts do you get a week, and how many of these are worth considering?

White: I have not kept a census on them. It's not an even flow from week to week. It's a seasonal thing. I would have to guess that a good percentage of the manuscripts we get are from students, highschool and college, and that what is going on in their year influences their production rate and when they stick the stories in the mailbox. So we get great loads of them at certain times of year and thin loads at other times. I would suppose we average five hundred a month. When I was assistant editor for *F&SF* we were averaging six hundred a month. I think *F&SF* got more, but I'm not sure of that. I did work out the percentages at *F&SF*, and this was the only time I ever did it. One story in six hundred would make it into print, because we were getting about six hundred a month and we were doing about one a month from the slush pile.

Q. Of the ones you receive, how many are worth considering at all and how many are illiterate rewrites of *Tarzan on Mars?*

White: I would suppose that better than fifty percent of the stories we get are marginally acceptable, marginally readable. They're stories that don't have a big glaring fault. It's not like the person can't handle grammar or has no ideas or is two years old or something. It's more subtle than that. It's a case where the prose somehow plods a little too much. The story isn't quite interesting; the idea isn't really fresh, hasn't really got any new insights in it, or it's simply dull. I would say the bulk of the stories we get fall in that category. It's sort of like a bell curve. In the middle, occupying the bulk of the curve of the bell, is this sort of acceptably mediocre level, and down on one end you have a few really fine stories and down on the other you have a few real stinkers of the first water, written by people who perhaps have hallucinations frequently or are otherwise living in another universe. [laughs]

Q. Do you find that when you're short of usable material you sort of dip into the bell a little bit?

White: No, it doesn't work that way. I have never had less than a year or half a year's worth of inventory to work with. I've gotten letters from people who've said, "Boy, you must have really had nothing to work with that month. You printed nothing but stories by people connected with your magazine. And they're all terrible. I know you didn't buy them because they were good stories but because they were connected with your magazine." These things aren't true. It just happened that time that his tastes really diverged from mine, but in truth I get about three good fantasy stories for every good science fiction story, so I'm heavily loaded with fantasy of all kinds, and when I see something I like I buy it. That's the way it usually works. Let's be candid. When I see something I like I accept it for purchase, and the money comes from the publisher at an undefined later date but usually before the magazine appears on the stands with the piece in it. Usually in fact when I schedule the piece for a given issue. At any rate I am not stampeded into buying something poor because I have nothing better. If you think I published something poor, this is because your tastes and mine diverged to a certain extent.

Q. What would you like to do with both of your magazines? What do you think should be done with a science fiction and a fantasy magazine?

White: I think that a great deal more money should be pumped into them. I think that they ought to have a full editorial staff, and their salaries should be of a competitive sort for the commercial world at large. I have actually worked this out with a possible backer. I feel that we could do with five salaried employees, which would include a production staff, which would enable us to incorporate a good deal more graphic design. I would pay top rates for stories. Everything would be sped up enormously in terms of the time it took us to do things. We'd have a superior package and we could put a superior price on it. I think about $1.25 for a magazine that has about 90,000 words of material in it, at least 70,000 of which are fiction. I would publish it *Vertex* size— not the tabloid *Vertex* but the earlier slick size, although my graphics would be quite different from theirs.

Q. Do you think that if you tried this the magazine would even survive? You'll notice that all previous attempts to publish science fiction magazines in this 8½x11 format have been resounding failures. *Analog* lost 20% of their circulation when they tried it. They got placed in a different part of the newsstand and science fiction readers didn't know where to find it.

White: No, that's not true. *Analog* to begin with was published in a format which was somewhat larger than the *Vertex* format at a time when a niche on the newsstands which now exists did not exist, and that is the *Creepy/Eerie* niche which has also Marvel's SF comic mag. I think that if *Amazing* and *Fantastic* were both in that size they would help reinforce the niche in which they appeared, and frankly my plans would not stop with them. I would want to do several magazines. One of them would be *Fantastic Adventures* revived as more of a straight sword and sorcery sort of fantasy magazine. I might even do another one, called something like *Heroic Fantasy*. I would probably do one that was a contemporary series character of the Doc Savage type. Right now I'm involved in doing such a series character for Pyramid Books. It's a brand new series called Doc Phoenix.

Q. What is he like?

White: Well, I can't tell you too much about it right now. He's first going to appear in a collection of new pulp stories that will be published by Pyramid in September or October, and he's there in an 8000 word story, which is a very uncomfortable length in which to introduce a new character and have a pulp story take place. He would then be appearing in a novel of his own, which I'm writing this June and which will be published about a year after it's finished.

Q. What exactly do you mean by a "pulp story"? Many people claim this is a false category and it only has to do with the kind of paper you use.

White: No, that's not true at all. The pulp story is something which evolved in its highest form to Dashiell Hammett and John D. MacDonald. I would say that John D. MacDonald is probably the finest flowering of pulp writing. By pulp writing I mean really good storytelling with involving, interesting characters doing things which involve in many cases action. That's considered to be synonymous with it. Good pulp fiction never pauses long enough for you to figure out whether the story is going in the right direction or not. It's just a relentless forward push. You can find this in the works of the best Western writers, people like Lee Hoffman for instance. This is unique to pulp fiction. You won't find it in "mainstream" or "literary" fiction. It's regarded as improper somehow. I think it reached its flowering in one form in the early Doc Savage that was written by Lester Dent, the man who wrote a million words a year and who was readable, unlike say Walter Gibson who wrote an 80,000 word Shadow novel every two weeks, and by God they're just about as boring as you could possibly imagine. To get back to magazines,

I would like to do a magazine devoted to a contemporary Doc Savage type character. I think it could be done without getting into all this Executioner or Killer shit that's on the newsstands now.

Q. Would it work, or haven't the comic books sort of usurped the market for this sort of thing?

White: I feel that there are a lot of kids reading comic books who are looking for something that gives them what comic books give them, but is working on a higher level. This is precisely what the series character pulps did in the thirties and forties, *Doc Savage*, *The Shadow*, *Phantom Detective*, and all the rest of them. I think this explains the success of their paperback reincarnations. If magazines were priced competitively with the expensive comics, which are going at a dollar a copy, and had good long involved and interesting stories in them—novels—around characters of that sort, with or without capes and costumes, there would be a built-in market for it. An actual progression above comics.

Q. Today kids looking for something like that go to a paperback store and buy Doc Savage. How would you teach them to look to the magazine rack?

White: If it's sitting right next to *Creepy* and *Savage Sword of Conan* and the rest of that I don't think they'd have a hard time finding it. I'm envisioning magazines which would be superficially similar in format. They'd be the same size and the ones that are more pulp oriented would have a more pulp oriented graphic package. I think it could be done in ways that won't be offensive. I'm not talking about the eight and ten year-old kids, but the thirteen, fourteen, fifteen year-olds, the ones who are already a little embarrassed to be seen reading comics of the cheaper sort, and who are buying the dollar comics with sex in them. [laughs] So, you know, they're ready for it. We don't live in a 1930s culture anymore. Your average teenager today is having sex, knows all about it, reads as much porn as he cares to. You don't have to shelter him. Give him something interesting to read.

Q. How do you think the writers will react when a market like that opens up? There's always the stigma that somebody who writes for a magazine like that is a "Hack" and not an "Artist" and so forth.

White: Well, some people get off on it. Some people who enjoy it. There are plenty of people who really enjoy writing smooth-moving, fast-reading fiction, and take a certain perverse pleasure, a reverse snobbery from the fact that they're not literary. I wouldn't want to categorize her as being extensively that way herself, but Lee Hoffman is rather like that. Lee Hoffman is a very modest, unassuming person about her own writing, and yet it's superbly good. It's won awards in the western field. Movies have been made of it. I think she'd have a lot of fun writing for a market like that. She and I were once working with Gil Kane on—the thing they did one issue of—I think it was *Call Him Savage*. It was one of Gil's attempts to elevate the comic book to a higher level. It ended up with Lin Carter doing something and he rewrote it.

Q. Who rewrote what?

White: Gil had his own conception of what he wanted. He fed it to Lee and me. We thought we knew what he wanted, and we worked up a treatment and gave it back to him, and he said, "No, no, this isn't at all like what I wanted." He told us all over again what he wanted and it was entirely different that time, so we worked something entirely different for him. It still wasn't what he had in mind. He realized he wasn't getting to us on that level, so he went over to Lin Carter and asked Lin to work it up for him, so Lin worked it up for him, and he said "Lin, this isn't what I had in mind at all." Ultimately what he did was loosely base it on what Lin had given him and mostly on his own writing, because he was the only one who knew what he had in his head. He couldn't really verbalize it.

Q. I did an interview with Norman Spinrad in which he mentioned something Mike Moorcock said, to the effect that if Adolf Hitler hadn't been Adolf Hitler he would have been a good sword and sorcery writer. What do you think of these claims that pulp hero fiction, with a superman who triumphs over all with little feeling or effort, is sort of crypto-Nazi, not good for you, and all that?

White: I think that's bullshit. Frankly, pulp fiction is somewhat infantile. It reflects a childish idealism. It appeals primarily to adolescents and pre-adolescents, and people who have preserved some of the feelings they had as adolescents. I don't think that's particularly bad. I don't think it's particularly Nazi-ish. Children see the world in pretty simple good/bad terms. They want to see the good guys win. They're perturbed when the good guys do not win. They would like to see a more consistent and ordered universe in which when somebody did something bad somebody who is good can go and sit on him. Heroes reflect an adult preoccupation with exactly the same notion. Whether they're sports heroes or war heroes or whatever, they're people who somehow have been able to simplify life to the point where winning something can be equated with really accomplishing something of great importance. You get it down to the point where you either win or lose, with a specific contest with rules and an end. We're very disturbed right now because wars used to more or less function that way, and now they don't. Viet Nam was most upsetting to us because it didn't follow the rules, and it didn't end, and it didn't end with us winning or losing. It petered out. It shifted ground. It slipped out from under us. Well, that's the way reality sometimes is but people even if they're forced to accept it don't have to like it. They want something that they can like. That's the appeal of escape fiction in all its forms, whether it's a fairy tale, or a story about somebody who is a hot rod racer, or whatever turns you on and allows you to escape from whatever doesn't turn you on. It's your entertainment.

Q. Do you think that the resurgence of escape fiction now, and the popularity of it during the Depression, show that when the world isn't going right people turn to fiction to forget it?

White: Well, let's not say that people are escaping in any permanent sense. It's not like they're becoming catatonic and comatose and locked out of the real world of problems and what-not, it's that after eight to ten hours of real world they want an hour or two of vacation from it. They know they've got to come back to it but they want something else that feels better for a while, whether it's being able to go to bed with somebody, or whether it's listening to music, or taking a drug, or reading, or going to the movies, or TV. All these things are legitimate forms of taking a vacation from unpleasant aspects of reality. There's nothing morally wrong with them. They help you cope and when we exist in times of great social stress, and it's not an upward pointing stress but a downward pointing stress, these things help us keep our wits. They help us from staying so depressed from life around us that we commit suicide or something equivalent. I think we're entering into a period like that, for sure. It seems that things move in cycles like that, up and down, down in the 1930s. But even in the Thirties people were basically optimistic about the future, and we're not optimistic about the future. We *know* that the future is going to be worse than the present. We have the evidence of our senses that the present is worse than the past, and therefore the future will be worse yet. It's hard to imagine that the future will get better in any one particular. We already know that it's going to be more crowded, that there are going to be less resources, that things we've been able to take for granted will be scarcities. This is just inevitable. This bums a lot of people out, and they want something they can turn to which will at least help them endure it.

Q. Isn't there a danger of overusing or abusing that sort of thing?

White: Any drug can become an opiate, so to speak, if it's used exclusively. There are people who drink four or five gallons of water a day and are inebriated through dillution of the blood, and they are known, believe it or not, as hydro-olics. You can do anything to excess. You can do reading to excess. I've known many people who didn't do much living because they spent all their time reading. I don't see as many of them anymore, though, as I do people who spend all day at the movies. Movie freaks seem to have replaced book freaks to a large extent. There are plenty of bored housewives who watch too much TV. People can certainly abuse anything they can enjoy. Anything you can get something out of you can get too much out of.

—*Disclave, May 1975*

80

Jack Williamson

Q. You first appeared in print in 1928. What was the science fiction field like then as compared to now?

Williamson: About as different as could be. In 1928 the term science fiction had not yet been invented. Hugo Gernsback called it "scientifiction" and *Amazing Stories*, the first all science fiction magazine, had just been started in 1926, two years before, and there were just a handful of people writing new science fiction in those days. Now *Amazing* in the beginning was a reprint magazine, reprinting Edgar Rice Burroughs and A. Merritt, Wells and Jules Verne and so forth, and just a handful of people such as Ed Hamilton and myself were doing new science fiction then.

Q. Were you at this time aware that there had been science fiction writers prior to the Gernsback period, in the slicks of the 1890s? Sam Moskowitz has reprinted a lot of this material recently. Did these writers influence you or did you find yourself starting out fresh?

Williamson: I had only a limited access to earlier science fiction, but the stories that Gernsback was using were reprinted and I came across people like Wells on the library shelves, and some SF things such as Mark Twain's *Connecticut Yankee* and Edgar Allan Poe, and some of Hawthorne's early stories. Basically I knew little about science fiction at the time; it was a wonderful new world for me when I discovered it.

Q. So basically you would say that science fiction as we know it started with Gernsback and *Amazing* and has no continuity before that?

Williamson: Well, that's not quite accurate because Burroughs was established with his Mars stories, and A. Merritt was tremendously popular in *Argosy*, and Wells had written his great science fiction. It was around,

81

but it wasn't named and identified as a pulp genre. What Gernsback did was invent a name for it and put it in specialized magazines. In some ways this was good and in some ways it was bad, because it got labelled as "pulp" stuff and got into a sort of ghetto from which it began to escape in the 1940s probably.

Q. Do you think that Gernsback did more harm than good? In my opinion at least the pre-Gernsback science fiction was far superior to anything published in the science fiction magazines until about 1940. You'll notice that it was possible to sell science fiction to, say, *Harper's* in 1910, but it wasn't possible again for thirty years.

Williamson: I'm not sure Gernsback was entirely to blame, but that was a low period in the history of science fiction. Why before the Gernsback period science fiction was not labelled with this ghetto label. It was either literate or it wasn't. Occasional writers were writing occasional science fiction, such as Conan Doyle and Wells, and the science fiction that was published was generally defensible on good literary grounds, and after SF got established as a labelled commodity, anything with that label on it could be sold for something. The field expanded tremendously, but I'm afraid the average quality went down.

Q. Then isn't it a good thing that today the definitions are breaking down?

Williamson: I think so. I think that instead of one field or one market we have a dozen or more today. It's a good thing. Why not?

Q. When you were writing science fiction in the 1930s and 1940s, was there any inherent difference between the way you put it together as opposed to now?

Williamson: The technique was pretty much the same. But literary standards have changed, the requirements of editors have changed; because Gernsback wanted scientific explanations in the stories and you could let things wander a little while you stopped the story to explain what was going on. This sort of thing was possible and generally the writers, the editors and the readers tended to be a little younger and a little less educated then than they are now. At least some SF nowadays is of higher literary quality.

Q. In order to survive from the Gernsback period to the present you had to be very adaptable. How did you get by when you found that the kind of thing Gernsback wanted didn't sell anymore?

Williamson: Well, I try to keep learning and changing. I don't know how to do it, except it's a matter of staying alive and doing new things. I suppose meeting the competition.

Q. John Campbell, during his editorship of *Astounding/Analog*, retrained a lot of writers to write more modern science fiction. Did he heavily influence what you were doing?

Williamson: He certainly did, but he did it more indirectly than directly. I read his magazine and knew him pretty well, and he used to write long letters, but I was part of the field when it was changing and growing. I was reading the stories that Campbell wrote as Don A. Stuart [the pseudonym under which he produced such classics as "Twilight" and "Who Goes There?"] and the stories from people like Heinlein and de Camp and Sturgeon and the like. I was reading those stories and I felt part of the field or genre or movement, and it was something new and exciting that was happening, and I was certainly influenced, but I felt that I was part of the whole thing.

Q. Also at this time you branched out into fantasy. Do you prefer it to science fiction; did you write it for the opportunity, or what?

Williamson: Well, I certainly enjoyed the fantasy I did. Part of it was done for John Campbell when he was publishing *Unknown*. I also used to write for the old *Weird Tales* and tremendously admired Farnsworth Wright who was the editor of it, and I think that the distinction between science fiction and fantasy is not as important as most people think. It's important in the background and the beginning of a story, but if the story works, once you get into the writing of it, the distinction melts away.

Q. It seems to me that the only working distinction is that in science fiction you are talking about a real possibility, something you think may happen, while in fantasy you are not.

Williamson: That's the distinction, and it's a matter of what people believe or what seems to be possible. The assumptions don't always square with the reality. For example, we used to write about jungles on Venus and we don't anymore.

Q. Do you usually write something because you think it is seriously possible, or because it works in a story?

Williamson: I like to have something that is seriously possible. That is I am inclined to believe that science fiction can be used to explore alternatives, and I take pains to try and fit a story into scientific possibility, but once a story gets going it takes on sort of a life of its own. The essential thing is to believe in a story, and when it's based on real science it's easier to believe in it. If I can believe in a fantasy, why it works just as well.

Q. How do you get a story started? Do you come up with a character and a situation, or a scientific concept, or a scene, or what?

Williamson: In many different ways I am inclined to think that I start out with an idea or a theme or a generalization, something abstract and work from this general abstraction or concept toward specific characters, specific incidents and scenes and so forth. It's a matter of working from the general and the abstract to the specific and concrete.

Q. When you write, especially in the case of a longer work, do you outline it first, or just sit down and write and see where it goes?

Williamson: I tend to outline it first. I think better when I'm outlining it. It forces me to make choices and decisions and so forth. But once it gets going I often depart from the outline. I like to start something, to write a few pages of a short story or a few chapters of a novel, then stop and discover what the theme is and where it's going, what the prominent mood is and when it's necessary to recast the outline and the interests of greater unity and purpose.

Q. Do you think that your stories, since they hold up as stories, will survive without dating? I notice that your first story has been reprinted many times recently. Do you think that all your work will hold up like that after as many years?

Williamson: I think by and large they do, or at least some of them do. Recently I've been putting together a book called *The Early Williamson*, which Isaac Asimov persuaded Doubleday to do. And in doing that I reread all my first stories, and was surprised that at least a few of them seemed to be very little dated, even scientifically. Of course there are some of them that have tropical jungles on Venus and so forth, so some of them are a bit dated, and sometimes the style is a little leisurely by today's standards, but let me say that if it was a story I was really excited about, that I felt had a strong emotional tone when I wrote it, why it seems to hold up pretty well, at least for me.

Q. Do you think the stories you are writing now will hold up as well in the next few decades?

Williamson: That's impossible to say. I hope so.

Q. Well, which of yours are your favorites, and are these the ones the readers liked?

Williamson: Well, I think so. There is a story called *Darker Than You Think*, a sort of half fantasy that's always been a favorite of mine and the readers I think have liked it well enough. Incidentally it has been suddenly quite successful in a French translation. And there's my old *Legion of Space* series which seems to have done pretty well. My most successful thing is a story called *The Humanoids* and that is one I don't feel quite as well about as I do, say, *Darker Than You Think*, because I feel that somehow it's a little ambiguous and incertain in the thematic impact.

Q. Well, it's now considered a classic. How does it feel to be a classic?

Williamson: It's wonderful being a classic.

Q. Are you still writing actively?

Williamson: I'm a full-time professor, which means the writing has to be pretty well limited to vacations and so forth, and I spent a month in Asia this summer which cut down the writing time, but I still keep things going. I am doing things on my own, and also in collaboration with Fred Pohl.

Q. What works haven't we seen yet?

Williamson: Well, I have a series of novelets that are supposed to go together to make a novel called *The Power of Blackness,* and the first of these was published in *The Magazine of Fantasy & Science Fiction* about a year and a half ago, and I'm just completing the fifth which will close the series. And I have another trilogy with Fred in progress, and the first of these has been published as magazine stories in *Galaxy* and *If,* and Ballantine Books is going to publish the first volume, I think in February, as *The Farthest Star.*

Q. By now you are probably the best person around to observe trends in science fiction. In what direction is the field heading now? Following the trends from practically the beginnings to the present, what do you think the future of SF is going to be like?

Williamson: That's hard to say, but it seems to me that one important thing in SF that I've seen since the beginning is a loss of faith in technology and science and man's reason and his own stature. I feel that we've had in recent years a sort of crisis of faith in science and in man himself. This reached its height in what is called "The New Wave" and I believe that there is now sort of a reaction against this, and there is more positive and less negative thinking about science and reasoning in the future than there was a few years ago. I feel that civilization is really in a desperate straight, but I think that we are more likely to deal with it if we approach it in terms of hope and reason than if we flee from it in panic.

Q. What about the impact of modern SF? More people are reading it than they were twenty years ago, when SF was more optimistic. Do you think this despairing attitude is going to do any damage, or is it simply reflecting current attitudes?

Williamson: I wonder if it doesn't help create current attitudes. It seems that there's maybe an element of accident in this, that bad news is more dramatic than good news, and that stories are easier to write and sell and are more interesting if they depict some appalling doom. And for that reason probably the dangers of technology have been somewhat exaggerated. This happens not only in science fiction but in science fiction movies and so forth, and this reaches a lot of people and it seems to me that maybe SF has tended to accelerate this crisis of faith.

Q. Where do you think this will come out? Will we get a reaction, and a reaction against science fiction at the same time?

Williamson: I hope not. I hope we can have a reaction in favor of a little more confidence in ourselves and our reason in the future, and a little more determination to solve our problems instead of running from them. It seems to me that one thing SF does is explore unlikely alternatives, but it is always prudent to look ahead and see where we're going and try to do something about it, and science fiction can certainly do that and has always done it and I hope it will keep doing it.

Q. What do you think was the impact of science fiction in the past? What was the impact of Gernsback with his extremely positive fiction, and Campbell with his slight shades of doubt? Did this influence anything?

Williamson: I'm sure it did, but it's impossible to accumulate any statistics. A lot of scientists have read science fiction, and *Astounding* used to sell out thousands of copies in Los Alamos and Oak Ridge where people were designing the atomic bomb. There's quite an interaction between science fiction and science, but you can't document the effects. Certainly science fiction is part of our popular consciousness, our popular culture, our popular mind, and it undoubtedly has effects.

Q. Thank you Mr. Williamson.

—Discon II, 1974

L. Sprague de Camp

Q. Lately there has been a tremendous revival of stories about brawnily thewed heroes, malevolent wizards and imperiled heroines. How do you account for this great barbarian revival?

De Camp: Well, it's partly a matter of accident. The big revival seems to have been sparked by the publication of Tolkien as much as anything. Of course when Tolkien came out in expensive clothbound volumes there weren't a great many of them printed, so for years there was simply the enthusiasm of a small circle of connoisseurs, as the Zimiamvian novels of Eric R. Eddison were some years previously. But when Tolkien was issued in paperback, and since it's an excellent story, it caught on, especially with the college crowd.

And another factor I think is that it's a reaction against the period of the reign of the anti-hero which featured in a great deal of fiction in the 1950s and '60s. You know, this wretched little jerk who has neither brawn nor brains nor character and can't do anything right. So he suffers and suffers like Ziggy in the cartoons. Well, Ziggy is all very amusing and in fact there are days when I feel a little bit like Ziggy myself, but nevertheless he's hardly what you would call a hero, and when people read fiction they usually like a character with whom they can identify.

The anti-hero, on the other hand, is constructed on the theory that no matter how poor or weak or stupid the reader is he can always say to himself, "Well, at least I'm better off than that twerp."

That sort of thing is all very well for a while, but people do get tired of it, so there arose a demand for people who really are heroes with a capital H. And the swordplay and sorcery genre has done what it could to fill that demand.

Q. What are the origins of heroic fantasy? What writers started it?

De Camp: If I knew the name of that writer I'd have to be good for time travel and go back to the stone age. As far as written literature goes it is ultimately derived from ancient myths and legends, hero tales like those of the Sumerian and Babylonian Gilgamesh, the tales of Homer and Vergil, the medieval romances and so on down. The medieval romance of course met a horrible fate. It was murdered by Miguel de Cervantes around the year 1600. You see, Cervantes had led a pretty rough, adventurous life himself. He'd fought in the battle of Lepanto where the Turks were beaten for the first time. He'd been captured and enslaved by the Barbary pirates, and he knew from painful experience that adventures are seldom so entertaining and sanitary as were the romances of gentle knights galloping around and rescuing maidens fair from vile enchanters and all that, so he wrote a hilarious burlesque, *Don Quixote*, and that so effectively ridiculed the romance that for a couple of centuries nobody cared to write any.

Then in the 18th and early 19th centuries fantasy gradually crept back into European literature through the peasant fairy tales collected by Han Christian Anderson and the Grimm brothers and others, the oriental extravaganza in the form of the *Arabian Nights* which were first translated into French in the early 18th century, and the gothic tale of supernatural horror which originated in Germany and was brought to England by Horace Walpole in his novel *The Castle of Otranto* in 1765. Then Sir Walter Scott with his invention of the modern historical costume romance in the early 19th century added another element, and in the latter part of the 1880s William Morris put all of these elements together into a series of romantic novels laid in an imaginary world where magic worked but machinery hadn't yet been invented. Then after him came Lord Dunsany, Tolkien, Eric Rucker Eddison whom I mentioned, Robert Howard, and other practitioners of the art. But it's only become what you might call really popular in the last decade with the paperback publication of Tolkien's *Lord of the Rings* series and the Conan stories of Robert Howard and several other persons, including myself.

Q. Do you think this is a viable form of writing, or just a passing fad?

De Camp: It's impossible to say how long the present enthusiasm for it will last. These things always go up and down. Around the time of the Second World War it looked as if fantasy in general had become a casualty of the machine age. There were practically no magazines successfully published in that field except for *Fantasy & Science Fiction*—No, *F&SF* didn't start until around 1950, and for a while there was almost no market for fantasy anywhere. But then it gradually revived and today it's a smaller market than straight science fiction but it's still a viable and living genre which may go on for a long time.

Q. Who do you think are the most important contemporary writers of heroic fantasy and why do you think they're important?

De Camp: Well, that's very hard to say. I could just list their sales figures, but that wouldn't prove anything because somebody who is popular this year may drop out of sight the next and somebody who has been struggling along just barely making a living may have a sudden success.

All I can do is tell you which ones I happen to like the best and that's my subjective opinion. I think very highly of Tolkien, of course. I enjoy Fritz Leiber's stories of Fafhrd and the Grey Mouser very much indeed and grab for one whenever I see it. I think very highly of Eddison although he's not a contemporary—he died in 1945. I have also enjoyed in varying degrees the stories in that field of Lin Carter, David Mason, and others. And Andre Norton, too. I'd forgotten about her for the moment. I think very highly of her work in that field. I'd put her pretty well on the top shelf.

Q. What about your own involvement in the field? How did you discover it or it discover you?

De Camp: The way I discovered it was back in 1939 when I was a relatively new freelance writer and I became acquainted with Fletcher Pratt. Pratt had the idea of doing a series of stories in which a modern character by the use of symbolic logic projects himself into various fantasy worlds, worlds of myth and legend. He wanted a collaborator so I undertook the job and we got started on the Harold Shea series, which is, of course, heroic fantasy or swordplay and sorcery before those terms came into use. And I've been at it one way or another ever since.

I had never heard of Robert E. Howard's Conan stories. In fact, I hardly knew who Howard was until 1950, I believe it was, when *Conan the Conqueror* was published in a clothbound edition and I read it and was hooked at once and read all the other stuff of Howard that I could get my hands on and then I had a part in the discovery of a number of unfinished manuscripts of Conan stories and some that had been written but not sold in Howard's lifetime, and I edited and rewrote and completed these various works and so I became more and more involved in the Conan business and am still in it.

Q. In the Conan stories you have written, what part of it is yours, what part is Lin Carter's and what part is the original conception?

De Camp: When a story is by Carter and myself the way we work is we get together and hash out a plot outline. That means sitting in a room with a pad and pencil—I usually do it because I can write shorthand—and we try out various ideas, and one will say, "Well how about this?" And the other says, "No, no that's too imitative. Mike Moorcock's already done that." "Well then how about having him do this?" "Oh that's too conventional. I tell you what, why don't we turn it upside down and have him do just the opposite and see what happens?" So we fool around that way for a while and finally we get a pretty good outline. Then I take it home and add a few details and I type out an extended synopsis of the whole story which usually runs to several pages of single spaced typing, and mail that to Carter.

Then Carter does the rough draft, which since Carter knows I'm going to correct is apt to be pretty rough, and sends that to me and I go through and do a second draft and get his approval on it—he may make some further changes—then send it out to a professional typist.

When Pratt and I collaborated we did it just the opposite: I did the rough drafts and he did the final drafts. You see, there is a reason for doing it that way, and that is that the younger writer is apt to be more fertile with ideas but the older writer is apt to be more critical and can spot the illogicality, the pieces of bad writing and things like that better than the younger man can. And we have checked that out, because when Pratt and I or Carter and I have tried to reverse the procedure it hasn't worked out so well and we both have gone back to the system I have described.

Q. Do you think there's any danger that the immense popularity of Conan will cause the entire fantasy field to be overrun with Conan look-alikes?

De Camp: Well, imitation is the sincerest form of flattery, of course, if you don't mind a cliche and, let's say that if other people imitate Carter and me we must be doing something right. Actually, almost any writer who makes any kind of splash is going to rouse up some imitators, and I try not to imitate my own predecessors but I know perfectly well that they're in there influencing me. Everything a writer reads, especially in his early years, is bound to influence him one way or another. And a seasoned writer should have assimilated these influences well enough so that they don't show.

For example, in my younger days I went through a Hemingway period because in the late 1930s Hemingway was the big noise. So my stories tend to show a definite use of the Hemingway short sentence dialogue and things like that. My erstwhile colleague, L. Ron Hubbard, once said, "Yeah, you know, the story runs like this: Jim walked down the street. He met Joe. He shot Joe. Joe fell. Joe died. Jim walked on. He walked into a saloon. He met Frank. He said to Frank, 'I've just shot Joe.' Frank said, 'Oh yeah?' Jim said, 'Oh yeah.'" And it goes on and on like that. Well, I did a bit of that I suppose too, and some of my other colleagues very definitely show where they have been through a Lovecraft period or a Howard period or a—I don't know, maybe somebody has been through a de Camp period by now. I haven't noticed any but it's possible.

Q. Have you had anything to do with the Conan comic books? They seem to be about to make Conan as well known as Tarzan. Do you think it's a good thing to get him that popular in that form?

De Camp: As far as I can make out the effects seem to cancel themselves out. I doubt if it makes any great difference, and on balance they probably help more than they hinder. The only dealings I ever had with the particular comic book company in question is that they did make a comic book out of one of my stories which had nothing to do with Conan, and that was "A Gun For a Dinosaur" and I thought they did a reasonably good job of it. I was rather pleased in other words. Also they paid me what they said they would which is always a help.

Q. Are you planning to write any more heroic fantasy in the near future?

De Camp: I should like to. That is largely a matter of finding a publisher who wants to publish it, because I don't write things on speculation anymore. But I should like to write the third book of the Jorian series, because the second was obviously left wide open for a sequel, and I have an idea for another trilogy laid in that same world, which, if I could find a publisher I might very well do.

Q. What are the market conditions for fantasy now?

De Camp: Oh, they go up and down. They are not so consistently favorable as straight science fiction, let's say, but on the other hand I get more fun out of writing fantasy.

I have done three novelets in the genre within the last year or so. I did one for Harry Harrison's Campbell memorial volume called "The Emperor's Fan." I did one for Carter's second *Flashing Swords* volume called "The Rug and the Bull," and I just did another one for him called "Two Yards of Dragon." It's about a noble young knight who goes out and slays a dragon and then is run in by the game warden.

Q. While we're talking about your fantasy, who do you think has influenced your fantasy writing more than anyone else?

De Camp: A good many people, starting with Edgar Rice Burroughs. And Tolkien, and Howard, and Thorne Smith who is not thought of much nowadays as a fantasy writer but he was one and a good one in his day. Such works as the one about the man who was turning into various animals starting with a horse, and *Skin and Bones* in which the man becomes an animated skeleton to the understandable dismay of his wife and associates. And there are several other people I could dig up if I gave the matter some thought.

Q. About the writing of fantasy now, do you think there is any inherent difference between the way you would write a fantasy story and the way you would write any other kind?

De Camp: No, not as far as I'm concerned. In a fantasy you make certain assumptions which are contrary to what we believe to be actual material facts on this Earth as of now. In other words without supernatural elements. And if we write a realistic story we stick to the laws of nature as we know them, and if we write a fantasy we make up a set of different laws. But we must stick to them once they are made up, so as to make the story internally self-consistent. No story that isn't internally self-consistent has much of a chance.

Q. What if the laws of nature as we understand them change? Suppose, for example, someone in the year 1000 A.D. were to write a fantasy story in which the world was round?

De Camp: That would really be a science fiction story I think, because it doesn't really involve a supernatural element, you see. No gods, demons, witches on broomsticks, elves, gnomes, spells, astrological prognostications or anything of that sort.

Q. Well, today many people believe in astrological prognostications. Would you still consider that fantasy?

De Camp: Well, let's say that's sort of borderline. Astrology is a pseudoscience. It was invented by the ancient Babylonians who didn't know any better and thought that the heavens were a glass bowl, and the earth was an island floating on water in the bowl, and the bowl kept turning over and over. The gods lived in bright little movable houses on wheels on the inside of the bowl, you see, which were the planets, and so when a planet was rising obviously that god's influence would be strong. When Mars (or Nergal as they called it) was rising because it was red and therefore suggested blood and fire there was likely to be war, and people have gone on that way ever since.

Well, of course most people do entertain pseudo-scientific or supernatural beliefs of one kind or another. There are very few conscious materialists in the world. But there is a fairly sharp distinction in the fictional field.

Q. Do you think fantasy has to be written in a way so that people at least half believe in it? When superstitions die out entirely will it still be possible to write fantasy?

De Camp: Oh, of course. I mean hardly anyone believes in witches on broomsticks anymore, but it's still perfectly possible to write a good story about them.

Q. Thank you Mr. de Camp.

—Discon II, 1974

Follow-up questions by Richard E. Geis:

REG: I'm never sure how to type your name. Is it DeCamp. . .De Camp . . .deCamp. . .de Camp?

de Camp: The name is de Camp, spelled with a lower case "d" save at the beginning of a sentence. I suppose that Laurent de Camp, when he landed in Staten Island in the 1680s used a little "d" since he was a Frenchman. Later generations Anglicised it to De Camp, but my paternal grandfather married a wife who thought that a little "d" would have more social cachet. This caused some hard feelings in the family. My great-uncle Clarence De Camp, of Boonton, NJ, refused to open a letter addressed to him as "de Camp." "Taint my name!" he said. I used to hate my name as a boy, but when I got into writing it came in handy, sounding more like a pseudonym than most real pseudonyms do. With a name like mine, who needs a pen name? But it does cause trouble when I travel abroad, since I never know whether hotel clerks and such people will file my mail under S, D, or C.

REG: Has the book of uncollected Lovecraft writings been completed for the publisher, Donald Grant? Is it scheduled for release?

de Camp: The book in question, *To Quebec and the Stars*, was finished over a year ago and should be published soon.

REG: Since you've spent so much time and effort accumulating the mass of material on Lovecraft, do you plan any more books or writings about him?

de Camp: I have written three articles on Lovecraft (two published so far) and given one lecture on him. I expect to rewrite the article in *Fantastic Stories* for inclusion in *Literary Swordsmen & Sorcerers*. After that, it depends on circumstances and opportunity. I will certainly get all the spin-off I can from my work on him.

REG: Is there material you've seen concerning Lovecraft since you finished the Biography that would lead you to revise any conclusions or value judgements you made in the book?

de Camp: Only in a few very minor details. I hope to incorporate these in the paperback edition. For example, I meant to visit Father John T. Dunn in Portsmouth, Ohio, before I finished work on *Lovecraft*, but circumstances prevented. Father Dunn knew Lovecraft around 1914-17 in Providence, when Dunn was a plumber and both he and HPL were aspirant amateur journalists. Last May, Dunn told me his reminiscences of Lovecraft—how at meetings HPL sat staring straight ahead, save when he answered a question; and how the sister of a member of the club once, as a joke, asked HPL to take her out on a date. He said he would have to ask his mother, although he was in his middle twenties at the time.

REG: How have the sales of *Lovecraft—A Biography* gone? Is the book accomplishing what you hoped it would? Is Lovecraft being discovered or recognized in academe?

de Camp: Sales, in five figures, have been gratifying. I have seen some evidence of academic interest in Lovecraft.

REG: Are you working on a book now?

de Camp: At the moment I am editing and abridging *Lovecraft—A Biography* for paperback publication.

REG: Who will be publishing the paperback edition?

de Camp: Ballantine Books.

REG: Do you have any major works planned?

de Camp: The next book for which I have contracted is *Literary Swords-*

men and Sorcerers, a set of literary-biographical sketches of the leading writers of heroic fantasy.

REG: Who will be publishing it? And who are the leading writers of heroic fantasy?

de Camp: Arkham House. Morris, Dunsany, Lovecraft, Eddison, Barringer, Howard, Pratt, Smith, Tolkien, T.H. White; with briefer mention of Kuttner, Moore, Ball, Page, Hubbard, and Leiber. (I am confining this to writers producing S&S before 1940.)

REG: Have you ever found a publisher for the third book of the Jorian series?

de Camp: No.

REG: You mentioned an idea for another trilogy using the Jorian background world. Would you give us a glimpse of what that story would involve?

de Camp: Travel, adventures, the intractability of humanity in the mass, the pains of learning better, good intentions gone agley.

REG: Has the market for fantasy changed significantly since Darrell asked you about it?

de Camp: Not that I have observed, but I am not in a position to observe very keenly.

REG: In your view is there a need for more graphic realism in heroic fantasy, or is the genre unable or unwilling to sustain the strain? Is more realism inconsistent with the fantasy element? Can a heroic figure survive as a hero if he has a sex life, if he goes to the bathroom and if he genuinely bleeds and is fearful?

de Camp: It depends on the taste of the reader and how well the particular story is done rather than on the precise degree of realism in it.

REG: Thank you, Mr. de Camp.

—September, 1975

Frank Belknap Long

Q. Could you tell me how your writing career started? How did you get into this business?

Long: Well, I'm covering that, of course, in my forthcoming biography of HPL, and also in an introduction to my forthcoming collection of short stories by Doubleday, to some extent. In general I should say that I began to write just before I went to college, probably when I was about sixteen or seventeen, and I always had a bent towards the weird and supernatural, but I think that knowing Lovecraft from an early age, and certain experiences going back before that sort of helped to lead me in that direction. I was an early member of the United Amateur Press Association. Lovecraft was one of the guiding spirits there for two or three years. He always was interested in amateur journalism, but at that time he was president of the bureau of critics, and one of the most outstanding figures in amateur journalism. I first wrote an essay for a boy's magazine when I was about sixteen. It wasn't on the fantastic order at all; it was just a very brief thing, and an amateur journalist out west, Paul Campbell saw it, and he invited me to join the United Amateur Press Association. And then I wrote a somewhat Poe-esque type story called "The Eye Above the Mantel" which appeared in *The United Amateur*. That was the official organ of the UAPA. Lovecraft saw it and wrote me. He wrote me a long letter about it. He compared it to Poe's "Shadow" and was very flattering in his comments, and then I got into correspondence with Lovecraft, and I had correspondence with him for the next fifteen or seventeen years. And then between Lovecraft's first visit to New York City and his second visit which occurred about two years later, Lovecraft sold three or four stories to *Weird Tales*, and then he invited the owner of *Weird Tales*, Herneberger, to call one evening at my home, and Lovecraft praised my stories so highly that from that time on they were taken for *Weird Tales*. The editor at that time was Baird, and later it was Farnsworth Wright. My first story appeared in *Weird Tales* way back in 1924, and the first one just had an interior illustration, and the second one was illustrated on the cover. And from that time on I think I sold about thirty-five stories to *Weird Tales* over the next ten years. When the Gernsback magazines appeared I sold two stories to the Gernsback group, and then a few years later the newsstands were flooded with perhaps a dozen science fiction magazines, and I had stories in almost all of them, *Strange Stories, Thrilling Wonder, Future* and so forth. Those were the days when I was making kind of a semi-living by just writing for the magazines, although I supplemented my income in other ways by ghost writing and so forth. I even had a literary revision group going for a few years with Lovecraft, in which we revised stories for clients. Well, that's what happened earlier. I feel that I wrote some stories in those days which I like very much today. I think they're as good as all my recent things. I did write quite a few pulp stories which I don't even like to read today, but I wrote a great number of them and I appeared in almost all the early science fiction magazines.

Q. How much did Lovecraft influence you as a writer? I notice that your styles are not similar.

Long: Not too similar, no. The first stories I wrote I think I was more under the influence of Kipling and Conrad and so forth. I had as much interest in sea stories and adventure stories as I did in the supernatural. I divided my stories into two groups. Most of my early stories were either written for *Weird Tales* or they were a little bit on the pulpish order. But when Campbell brought out his *Astounding* and was the presiding genius there for a great number of years I probably wrote about thirty stories for those two magazines—*Astounding* and *Unknown Worlds* later—which I think were my best stories of that period. That type was called "the new science fiction," you see, and I think that from a purely literary point of view those stories stand head and shoulders above the stories I wrote for the eight or ten science fiction magazines, but there are a few of the *Weird Tales* stories, even some of my earliest ones, that I like just about as much. And they have been extensively anthologized. I've had about fifty stories in hardcover anthologies bearing the imprint of major publishers. Those are the stories, of course, of which I am most proud.

Q. Why do you think your *Weird Tales* stories are the ones that are the most remembered today?

Long: I don't know myself. Perhaps I was very youthful and exhuberant and I put all I had into them at the time and that's it. About one third of all my anthologized stories do go back to those early *Weird Tales* days.

Q. Do you think it has something to do with your association with Lovecraft?

Long: To some extent, there's no question. I think he was responsible for my getting into *Weird Tales* in the first place. My writing in those early years was undoubtedly influenced to some extent by my long association with Lovecraft. I don't think I ever came very close to his style but you will find little stylistic tendencies in all my early stories which I think could be thought of as Lovecraftian.

Q. Could you explain how you ended up writing one of Lovecraft's dreams as a story in *Horror From The Hills?*

Long: Well, he wrote me about this dream in a long letter, you see, and I was so impressed by it that I asked permission to incorporate it in *The Horror From The Hills.* Of course it's probably the strongest part of the novel. He gave a couple of other writers permission to do that but they never took advantage of it. I was the only one who ever included it in anything.

Q. Did he ever think of doing it himself?

Long: I don't think so. He had so many of those. He'd write in his letters so many of these dream visions that I don't think it ever occurred to him to incorporate that particular one. He just wrote it for entertainment, just to enlighten one of his correspondents. That's all it amounted to.

Q. What do you think of L. Sprague de Camp's claim in his book on Lovecraft that HPL never conducted himself as a professional to exploit his own potential fully? For example, a more professional writer would have written that dream up himself.

Long: Yes, but I don't blame Lovecraft for being the kind of writer he was. He was *not* a commercially oriented writer. He was an artist and this accent on material success and all that just didn't mean too much to him. He was his own worst enemy in that respect, but he was primarily interested in his art, in writing fine stories, and making a commercial success of it just wasn't important to him. That's true of all great artists, many of whom occupy paupers' graves because of that. Any of the great poets like Keats or any of the great musicians like Mozart and so forth, were primarily concerned with artistic creation. They were not successful business men. They didn't think to be or hope to be.

Q. Did you try and get him to make more of himself at the time?

Long: No, no, I never did. There was a rumor at one time that I tried to get him to study something on modern plot outlines and so forth, but he was having difficulty selling stories and I made that suggestion but he didn't take it seriously, and if he had taken it seriously it would have been very unfortunate. I've never tried to commercialize my work. When I write the story remuneration never even enters my mind. Of course I have always been faced with the necessity of selling them and made editorial contacts with that in mind, but when I actually sit down to write the stories then I don't give the commercial aspects a thought. Otherwise I'm sure my stories would be much worse than they are.

Q. Don't you think there was something terribly wrong when the man could leave novels, including his best work like *The Case of Charles Dexter Ward* unsubmitted and unpublished?

Long: Well, he wasn't a practical man, you see. He was like so many artists. All great artists have that side to their nature. Not all of them by any means, but it's very characteristic of the dedicated artist. They don't think of how much money they can make or how successful they can be. He thought of it; he would have liked money of course, but he was not nearly as frustrated and embittered and unhappy as you might suspect. I think Sprague puts a little too much emphasis on that. He had many moments when I think his lifestyle was just the right lifestyle.

Q. How did he impress you as a person when you first met him?

Long: Oh he was a very cultivated gentleman, you see, a very kindly man, a man of great generosity of mind. He wasn't out for himself at all.

Q. Do you ever worry about your own reputation for your own fiction being overshadowed by your association with Lovecraft?

Long: No, I don't think so. My work is different from his work. You see I think my supernatural horror stories, my fantasy stories, my science fiction stories, are not basically Lovecraftian. My stories have to be judged on their own merit as my stories.

Q. Don't a lot of people remember you today as just someone who knew Lovecraft?

Long: Not entirely. I've gotten some quite impressive critical praise for my stories. The fact that so many of them have been published by major publishers, in anthologies and that sort of thing indicates that I do have a reputation of my own. I want to do justice to Lovecraft. I want him to become even better known. I think he's a great writer and it's very important for anyone who knew him to write about him as much as possible.

Q. Your book on HPL, what is it going to be? Is it going to be a factual biography?

Long: It's going to be a little symbolical in a way. It's going to create an image of the man as he was in a larger sense, not just as you might think by a vast piling up of facts. I think paradoxical as it may seem, just facts piled on facts can be terribly misleading, as to both a writer's stature as an artist or just as a man. Therefore my book I think will be much more sympathetic, because I judge him as an artist. I almost brush aside his lack of commercial success and all that. I don't think that was a very important aspect of his character. I think it's splendid that there are a few men who regard this competitive struggle as unworthy of them.

Q. Have you ever tried to reconcile the seeming contradictions in him? For example, this very very uncommercial writer was perfectly willing to do ghost writing for people who were unworthy of his time.

Long: Well, he really did desperately need money at times. And then he wanted to help these people, and he was so generous that a young writer who didn't have any great talent he felt could be encouraged and improved across the years by literary advice and so forth.

Q. Well, if you look through the Arkham House volume *The Horror In The Museum* it would seem that none of those writers ever made it by themselves.

Long: No, he made a very great mistake, of course. I think he wasted too much of his talent on writers who had no great promise, who were third-raters.

Q. Might it not be that he did all the work for them by rewriting their stories rather than making them do it, so they never actually learned anything?

Long: I wouldn't say that exactly. I don't think they ever could learn in the majority of the cases. I mean they were not really gifted writers at all. Some of them did show promise though, and a writer can be very slow in his development. When he's very young he can write some very crude things, and just a few years later he can show exceptional promise. So Lovecraft saw that and he realized that in certain stories there was this promise, and he tried to cultivate it. And in a few cases where those writers were revised and encouraged, why they did achieve quite a bit. I can't think of any right off hand, but at least four or five of them have done quite well.

Q. He encouraged people like Robert Bloch, but he didn't actually rewrite their stories, like he did with, say, Zealia Bishop.

Long: No, but Bloch was a tremendously brilliant writer in his own right, you see. That was the point, and he recognized this great talent in Bloch when he first encountered him.

Q. It mentions in *The Horror In The Museum* that you had a hand in "The Mound."

Long: No I didn't. That was a mistake, which Sprague made and two or three other people made. I think Zealia Brown Reed made it herself in that little article that she wrote in one of the Arkham House books. No I didn't. I didn't have anything to do with it. She mentions that she had called on me in New York when Howard was present, and that she had turned "The Mound" over to me, you see. Actually Howard was not present at that meeting. She had met him two months before in Providence, and I was never given "The Mound" to revise.

Q. I notice that today a tremendous number of writers are trying to revive the Cthulhu Mythos and continue it. Do you think this is a good idea?

Long: I have no objection to it.

Q. Don't you think they sort of dilute everything? I mean four hundred *Necronomicons* are considerably less effective than one.

Long: Oh yes of course that's true in a way, and then so many of these young writers try to imitate Howard and they just take the things out of the books that are perhaps the worst aspects of his writing. I mean they use all his trite adjectives, his cliches. They use very trite adjectives, in some of the ones that are getting published quite extensively even. Some of them use phrases which to me are ridiculous. Old pulp drivel, like clutching hands and 'a shudder ran up my spine' and that sort of thing. The old cliches that seemed like cliches a century ago. Even in the days of Poe some of the writings contained phrases that seemed hackneyed. You see the trouble is in that kind of writing it's very difficult to avoid all those trite phrases, 'cold clammy hands at the back of the neck' and that kind of thing.

Q. It seems to me that what happens is that even writers with genuine talent get caught in sort of a straighjacket doing imitation Lovecraft with the last few lines in italics and everything.

Long: Yes, I think so, yes. Of course they lose the tremendous power of the original stories. All they get is this tendency which Howard had to pile too many adjectives on top of one another.

Q. Why do you think that the original ones were so powerful and the later ones are not?

Long: Well, it was the tremendous subconscious power that Howard had. It transcended all his defects of style, all the things with which you could pick holes in his stories, because his feeling for the supernatural, the weird and the strange and the cosmic, was so powerful that it simply transcended all those things.

Q. Would you agree then that it is not a good idea to write in the manner of someone else?

Long: Basically, that's right. It's very foolish, but all writers will do that, especially in their youth. I had various times years ago when I was imitating Arthur Machen, even Dunsany. I had my Dunsanian period. Of course I came completely under the influence of Poe when I was about seventeen or eighteen.

Q. What did you write in imitation of Dunsany? I've never seen any of it.

Long: Some of my poetic things. I once did a short prose poem for the old *United Amateur* that was very Dunsanian.

Q. Why do you think the supernatural horror story still has appeal today?

Long: It'll always have appeal.

Q. But this is a very materialistic age.

Long: Well no, in America for the last few years there has been a tremendous interest in the supernatural, all this occultism and that sort of thing. I don't believe in ghosts at all, and I don't believe in all these psychic manifestations that have impressed the young so much, but there is this tremendous interest in that sort of thing, and of course that is reflected to some extent on supernatural horror story writing.

Q. Why should supernatural writing necessarily be horror story writing?

Long: It doesn't have to be, no. I don't like the very gruesome stories, even though I've written a few of them myself. I try to avoid that as a rule, this absolute graveyard sort of thing. I think the best models are writers like Henry James in his *The Turn of the Screw* and the ghost stories of M. R. James, where the emphasis was on the more subtle elements of horror. Those are much more sophisticated stories in a much superior style.

Q. Did you ever think of writing a supernatural story in which there is no horror? For example, if a ghost were to walk into this room there's no reason why we should be afraid of it. We might just as easily ask it to sit down and tell us all about the afterlife.

Long: Well, I never tried to do a story of exactly that sort. I have a tendency in some of my stories to bring in Egypt and so forth, the horrors of the ancient world. But there's been an element of horror in all my supernatural stories, because it provides a certain stimulation. You see I'm not entirely a horror story writer. I've written a great many science fiction stories, light fantasies, humorous fantasies, and so forth. I would say no more than one fifth of my writing has been in that particular realm.

Q. How did you turn to writing science fiction? When you started we didn't really have science fiction as a *genre*.

Long: Well, I've always had a kind of bent for science fiction. I used to read Jules Verne when I was a kid, and all of H. G. Wells. I like science fiction. Also when science fiction became a much more promising field from the point of view of selling stories, I wrote more science fiction stories. I would have just as soon gone on writing primarily weird stories I should think, if there had been five or six magazines devoted to that sort of thing.

Q. What are you writing now? I noticed you did have one story in *Fantastic* recently.

Long: Yes, that's right. I think it's a very good story. It's a very recent story, and I wish I could have sold it for three times what I got for it, but the market for that sort of thing is very limited today, you see. It's mostly science fiction and to sell a novel or a short story in the supernatural horror realm, in most cases you have to give the story away.

Q. Since there is no market, is there any point in continuing to write this sort of thing?

Long: Oh yes, because it is important to me. Art and the creation of a story which is artistic and genuine is very important to me. I get more pleasure out of doing that than I do selling a story. But today I have written about nine gothic novels under my wife's name you see, Rita Belknap Long, published by Avon and Lancer and Belmont and Ballantine. I think they contain some of the strongest supernatural story writing I ever turned out, but they're buried in the whole gothic romance thing which never gets taken seriously by critics and the books are very seldom reviewed, and in the paperback field perhaps the majority of them are quite terrible, so as far as increasing your literary recognition is concerned it doesn't amount to anything. That has occupied me to some extent in the last few years because there is a tremendous demand for that sort of thing, and I can get an advance on a novel as soon as I send out a chapter or two.

Q. Why do you as an artist bother with something you're not going to get recognition for?

Long: In this case for commercial reasons. I mean, naturally I have to make a living. I would prefer to write science fiction stories but you have to write a complete novel in science fiction in order to sell it today, whereas there's such a demand for this gothic material that you write just a chapter or two and you get perhaps a thousand dollars advance. So I've been doing more of that in the last few years. It's a temporary thing. I don't expect to go on with it, but if I could be offered five thousand dollars for a science fiction novel I would drop everything and write a science fiction novel.

Q. Do you as the artist and you as the commercial writer ever find conflicts, or can you make this work well together?

Long: I think so, because I don't really do hackwork. I get involved in writing a novel, and I forget all about the remuneration. I never try to deliberately write to please editors except in rare instances. You have to do that occasionally of course. But in general I don't conform to an editor's ideas. I write to please myself and to make a story strong enough so that an editor will buy them even though they don't adhere strictly to formula.

102

Q. Do you think the field today is dominated by formula writers?

Long: Probably if I devoted more time to formula writing and studying what editors want I could perhaps make a fortune. At times I can turn out stuff in a very prolific way, you see. I have turned out four or five thousand words a day on occasion. But I just can't bring myself to it. I hate to study just what editorial requirements are. It disgusts me because it's so distorted in many ways. All they're thinking about is will this book sell and so forth. Too much appeals to a half-baked audience like some old woman who likes gothic romances but has never read a serious book in her life.

Q. Do you find this kind of formula requirement today in science fiction?

Long: To a much lesser extent than in some other field. The trouble is, you see, that about four or five of the top writers in the science fiction field have almost cornered the market, because they all happen to be extremely prolific, Bob Silverberg for instance is one, and Asimov of course was gone from it for many years but recently he went back. In general the publishers of science fiction get so many unusual novels written by five or six writers in the field that it's very difficult to sell a continuous series of stories to the science fiction paperbacks. The best field in that direction is of course the hardcover group but there's a problem there too because they sometimes take more than a year to bring a novel out, and you don't get too much advance on it and it may get reviewed on the front page of *The New York Times* and it may not sell very well.

Q. Thank you Mr. Long.

—Lunacon, April 1975

Gahan Wilson

Q. How did you come to specialize in cartoons mixing horror elements and humor?

Wilson: Well, I suppose that the two things combine quite nicely, the horror and the humor. If you make a monster, say in a movie, and you're successful, he's horrible. If you're not successful he becomes funny. You laugh at him. The two things are very closely related. They're not the same, identical thing; they're just seen from a different point of view. And as for how I got tied in in the first place, I just always had an innocent affection for the macabre.

Q. When you get an idea for a cartoon, how do you transfer it from your head to the paper? Do you make preliminary drafts?

Wilson: First I work out the basic idea, then I develop the thing, and once I get it to a stage where the general concept is clear then I make a little doodle in a notebook where I might put a whole bunch of ideas at once. I do it on a page, just one right after the other. So that's step one. I've got the idea nailed down and I have a memo to myself on it. When I actually go to do the cartoon it becomes a technical operation. I develop it and I sharpen it up, and I adjust little details so the idea will be exploited as much as possible, and it will be made so it communicates.

Q. How does this relate to your writing? You know the old bit about a picture being worth a thousand words. Do you find it easier to use most of your ideas as cartoons or stories?

Wilson: Since I do both cartoons and writing I find that the processes are really very much the same. Very often if you sit and think about a cartoon you'll see that it has an obvious series of events leading up to the cartoon you see and a series of events which will inevitably flow from the cartoon. So really you're taking the pivotal point in a story and that's what you're illustrating. That's really it. You've got a flash. It's the difference between an animated movie and a still. You've got a guy walking, and one way you see him walking and the other way you have him standing on one toe and the other foot's swinging out ahead. That's walking too.

Q. Have you ever thought about doing more involved cartoons? I've seen your one-page "Nuts" strip, but have you ever wanted to do a longer narrative, perhaps a supernatural thing, at comic book length?

Wilson: No, I have never gotten into that, the idea of doing a comic book type thing, the narration of a supernatural story. No.

Q. How about an underground?

Wilson: Maybe. That's a possibility. I've never been approached on it and I don't know. Somehow I don't think so. I've got other things that I am already doing and I think the underground thing is pretty well finished. I've seen some excellent stuff in the undergrounds but the statement has pretty well been made.

Q. Who are the influences on you, both as a writer and as a cartoonist? Can you separate them?

Wilson: Well, I can point to a lot of the ones that I'm aware of: W. C. Fields, Gogol, or Edgar Allan Poe, or Goya, Dick Tracy—a melange of stuff, you know, Bela Lugosi and Bram Stoker. They all influenced me, and some of them I very consciously studied. I very carefully observed what it was about the Frankenstein monster that made him look scary, the lighting, the way he moved, and so on, the little touch about putting those lids on Karloff's eyes that changed it from rather ordinary make-up into something terrific. Other influences have just sort of been absorbed, and I have no idea where they came from. I suppose some of them I could track down, and others I never could find.

Q. Do you like being compared to Charles Addams?

Wilson: It's certainly okay with me. Addams is, however, based very heavily on the 1930s movies, and I think I've gotten into more of a contemporary scene, and also more into social commentary. I have a thing which I generally say, which is that I started by being influenced by the gothics, *Dracula, Frankenstein,* and so on and lately I've been more heavily influenced by Walter Cronkite.

Q. You mean he can produce greater horrors than the imagination?

Wilson: Absolutely. Your standard television news show is more horrific these days than any of the gothics.

Q. Don't you think there's a difference between being *genuinely* horrific

105

and being pleasantly horrific, the way Bela Lugosi was?

Wilson: What do you mean—Lugosi was sort of pleasantly horrific?

Q. Well, he's something you want to go see, while you wouldn't care to meet, say, Adolf Hitler.

Wilson: Oh no. There's a definite difference. For example when I'm doing a cartoon the basic thing is that it should be funny. If it isn't funny I've failed. If I do a monster which just terrified you, or made you sick or something like that, I'd have blown it. What you have to do is take these horrors and end up being a joke, or it's not a cartoon.

Q. What kind of background do you have in cartooning? Did you go to art school?

Wilson: Yes I went to the Art Institute of Chicago and took a four-year Fine Arts course which was an excellent one, and it was both painting and drawing, and the graphics. I found that the commercial schools didn't teach you anything except very superficial stuff, so I went into Fine Arts. I've never regretted it. It's a good idea.

Q. How did you start getting cartoons into print?

Wilson: Just the usual. I went around and kept trying to sell them and eventually somebody bought them. I think that's really about what it amounted to. I just showed them to the editors, and at long last somebody picked them up.

Q. Who was the first to buy one?

Wilson: *Collier's* magazine.

Q. Then basically someone saw that and you got into *Playboy?*

Wilson: That's how, yes. Once you sell to your first major market then the other major markets believe you exist and that's how it goes.

Q. Do you think you'll ever become as well known as a writer as you are as a cartoonist?

Wilson: Yeah, I think it's quite possible.

Q. Do people notice your stories?

Wilson: Not yet, because I haven't written enough. I've been literally too busy. I have deadline things for the cartoons so I haven't done the stories. Now I've committed myself to Doubleday for a collection of short stories and I'll have to write a whole bunch to fill that commitment. That I hope will get me off and get me going. I'll just have to stick myself with the necessity of doing these things.

106

Q. You mean you're going to write a collection of supernatural and fantasy stories?

Wilson: Yes. It's sold, but it hasn't got a title yet.

Q. Are you going to do any more of those half graphic stories, like the inkblot story in *Again Dangerous Visions?*

Wilson: I don't think so. Ellison thought that up and I thought it was sort of a cute idea, but I don't know how far I'd want to fuddle with it. I doubt it seriously. I might if I get some bright ideas, but I don't think so.

Q. How long does it take you to draw a cartoon? You mention having your time all taken up—how long does it take to do a one-page color job?

Wilson: A one-page color job? It takes me, I'd say, all told a good three days. That's counting leaving it around for a third day and sort of studying it off and on.

Q. One thing that's always kept me out of the graphic arts is that I haven't the patience to spend three days on one little piece of paper.

Wilson: Well, patience is absolutely a prime requisite.

Q. Do you do it in stages, such as a simple drawing, more complicated shading, and such, or all at once?

Wilson: I do it by stages in that I start out with a line drawing and then I color in the basic colors and I proceed to the subtleties and the like.

Q. What do you do if you're half way through and discover you want to change something? Do you have to throw the whole thing out and start over?

Wilson: Sometimes.

Q. Do you ever sell cartoons to editors the way a novelist sells three chapters of a novel and a synopsis?

Wilson: No. It doesn't work that way. You do what you call a rough, which is the drawing with the cartoon in it, and that's it. There would be no way to sell a cartoon unless you have the whole idea.

Q. The editor then tells you which roughs he wants?

Wilson: Right. In one sense that's it. For example I sell a cartoon that takes place in an office. The editor knows I can draw an office, so I just indicate very, very briefly that there is an office, or maybe I don't even indicate it—there's a secretary, so obviously there's an office—but for the finish, certainly for a *Playboy* color finish, it is understood that there will be an office shown in detail. So in that sense, yeah, they're buying the thing knowing that I'll fill in all the rest of the stuff.

Q. Do you feel differently about illustrating as opposed to drawing your own ideas?

Wilson: I've abandoned illustrating because, for one thing it's not your book and I'd rather just do the whole book. That's it. I'm finished with illustrating.

Q. Will you illustrate your own books?

Wilson: Oh yeah. I'm doing children's books. I've got one out called *The Bang-Bang Family* with Scribners and I've got a series also with Scribners called *Harry The Fat Bear Spy*, and they are illustrated by me. The second one I'm illustrating now, and it'll be called *Harry Meets The Sea Serpent*.

Q. How is the writing different for writing a children's book?

Wilson: It's not all that different. You're writing for a specific person, an audience type. When you write for a grown-up you're talking as you talk to a grown-up. When you're writing for a child, you're writing for a child. But you're writing respectfully at all times. You know, I hate the goo-goo sort of talk to a child. You talk to the kid appreciating that he's a human being and full of responses and subtle and so on, but you don't bring in references to some grown-up junk because the kid wouldn't understand it. It wouldn't communicate.

Q. You mean you don't bring in a lot of factual data?

Wilson: Well, kids know lots of facts, but there would be no point in telling a kid about the fatigue of a job and working with an employer and union problems, and that sort of stuff. Sex, you know—going into sex. So you talk about the things the kid is into, you know, school and so on.

Q. Do you find that kids have a different sense of humor?

Wilson: I think kids probably have by and large a simpler sense of humor more direct, and the frame of reference is narrower than in an adult, but they're quick. They're very, very quick, and as I say it's just essential not to condescend to them because they'll spot it at once. They see through fakery. For example it's almost impossible for a magician to do tricks for kids, because they don't buy misdirection. You can tell an adult, "look at this hand," holding that hand up and they'll look at your hand, but do that with kids and they'll certainly see your other hand go back and get the silk handkerchief out of your hip pocket.

Q. Do you find that the juvenile audience and the adult audience overlap very much?

Wilson: No. I don't. The children's books I do are definitely aimed at children. The only adults who are likely to read them are adults with children who are reading them to the kids.

Q. You mean they're written for smaller children?

Wilson: Yeah, they're written for kids.

Q. Thank you Mr. Wilson.
—1st World Fantasy Convention, October 1975

Jerry Pournelle

Q. You're presently considered one of the more promising new "hard science" writers—

Pournelle: People who like hard science seem to like the stuff I write. I rank first or second consistently in the readers' poll in *Analog*. I very seldom write a story that doesn't get a bonus. If you like hard science you like my stuff. If you don't you can't stand it.

Q. What is the appeal of this sort of story?

Pournelle: There are a lot of people who like science fiction stories in which the science makes sense, the assumptions go by the rules, in which the writer knows what he is talking about, and doesn't do things like have a computer capable of ressurrecting people after they've fallen over a hundred-foot cliff but can't cope with a rusty knife, as in one of Harlan's stories. Now I'm not knocking Harlan's stories—he's a better word painter than I am, but he's a rotten scientist. His stories aren't even internally consistent, but he paints beautiful images. I think there's a market for the kind of [word] painter who can paint a consistent true to life picture, as opposed to abstract painting that gives one an emotional appeal without any intellectual content. You see what I'm getting at? The emphasis in what I write is on the intellectual, not the emotional, basically.

Q. Do you build your stories out of concepts or out of characters?

Pournelle: All stories are about people. If there are no people in it it isn't a story; it's an article. So to that extent they all have to do with characters. But I guess that you would have to say that for me and for Larry Niven, and for some of the others in the nuts and bolts business, the concept and the story-line are more important than the characters.

110

It doesn't mean that we neglect them, but maybe we put more emphasis on the story than we do on the people.

Q. Do you consider "hard science" to mean only physics, astronomy, etc.? Or do you draw from other areas as well?

Pournelle: Well, I've been a successful campaign manager. I have put several people into the congress; I have elected several mayors. I know something about the way the political process works, which I think is not true of most science fiction writers. So then in most of my stories the politics work. At least they make sense. The ways people act in my stories are not significantly different from the ways people act in the real political world, as opposed to a lot of science fiction stories in which they populate planets with angels, people don't act the way they normally do. They act the way the writer wants them to. Every utopia works marvellously in a novel, but damn few of them work well when you have to go out and people them with real live human beings who are cantankerous, have mother-in-laws who bother them, and so on. People have a habit of being a lot more ornery than most writers want them to be when they write social science fiction.

Q. Are you assuming then that human nature will always remain constant whatever the situation? Couldn't you write a story in which the society is so different that people behave differently, and are not as ornery?

Pournelle: I guess what we would have to say is that for about twenty thousand years that we know of human nature hasn't changed very much, and consequently it is hard to convince me that it is going to change a great deal in the next five hundred. It *could*, but if it does it will be the result of somebody really and deliberately manipulating people, and that itself has consequences because the guy doing the manipulating now *knows* that the only value in this world is power; he's got it —I mean there's a whole literature of the philosophy of power. Probably the best example is C. S. Lewis' book, *The Abolition of Man*. Mankind to some extent depends upon the concept that there is something beyond man that is worth striving for. It is wrong to kill children and eat them. No really, you can't intellectually defend that proposition. Why shouldn't you kill kids and eat them? Kill your own and eat them if you're hungry. Why not? But the concept of mankind as we know mankind depends upon the fact that it is just wrong to do that, that there is something beyond us. Let's take a vote on it. Everybody in the room votes, yes, let's eat this guy. It's still a wrong thing to do, whether we agree to it or not. Now if you have gotten to the point where I can put into you a completely different value by simply pushing buttons or manipulating switches, what it does to you is not half so significant as what it does to me.

Q. You mean you become God, and remake mankind?

Pournelle: Or maybe I become a man who knows there is no God, which is even worse. I don't mean a man who suspects there isn't one, who says there isn't one—I mean a man who knows there isn't one. And you don't meet very many people who *know* there is no God. You meet a lot of people who say it, who claim it, who'll intellectually argue it and say "May God strike me dead thirty seconds from now if he exists" and call this proof that he doesn't, but you don't meet many people who act as if there isn't a set of rules for behavior. You don't meet very many people who because the children in the house next door are annoying with their laughter set fire to the house and kill them. Yet logically, intellectually, why shouldn't he do it? He can get away with it and not get caught, it won't endanger his house. Why shouldn't he kill the kids next door when their laughter disturbs him?

Q. Isn't it possible that some command against killing at random or eating your neighbor's kids is built into the species as a survival value, not a higher value but an instinct.

Pournelle: If that is the case that's fine, but it is then what I call the nature of Man and maybe we justify it by appealing to higher law and theological arguments and so forth. But what I'm trying to get at is if you come up with the ability to take that instinct out of people, so that Man becomes infinitely maleable, so that I can take you and turn you into anything I want you to be, the important consequence is not, I suppose, what happens to you in that situation but what happens to *me* when I know that for sure because I have become a monster, not a man. You've become less than a man, and I've become even less than you.

Q. Have you ever thought of writing a story about that?

Pournelle: I've done it, and I'm doing some more. Sure, and one of these days I'm going to write a regular mainstream novel about a guy who lives in what you might call a logical anarchist manner. If people annoy him he kills them. If he can get away with it. If he can't get away with it he doesn't do it because he doesn't want to go to the electric chair, but if he can get away with it the hell with it. The school next door—the school children bother him during recess. Burn the school down. What kind of a man is that? Is it a man? What does it do to a man to think that way and to have that kind of a set of values? Or rather, I should say, the absence of values. I'd call that a hard science story.

Q. Then how would you define a hard science story? We've thrown the term around a bit.

Pournelle: A story which is consistent about what is scientifically known about the subject matter of which you are writing.

Q. Wouldn't that disqualify all stories involving faster than light travel?

Pournelle: Well, again science fiction is allowed traditionally a couple of false to fact assumptions.

112

Q. Not always. When Jules Verne invented his Moon-cannon, at least *he* thought it would work.

Pournelle: I see what you're trying to get at. Well, in the old—maybe I'm taking you back a ways, but as recently as twenty years ago science fiction was said to be allowed to make a couple of assumptions like, now suppose something can work that is now thought can't, then what would happen? If this happens, then what? If you used a whole slew of them, forty or fifty of them, you were writing the kind of stuff that Doc Smith used to write, the space opera. Traditionally hard science fiction was based on only one or two assumptions that were false to what was known then to be fact. I don't happen to be convinced that there is no such thing as faster than light travel. I can think of at least a couple ways it can be accomplished. As a matter of fact there are a pair of chaps named Lee and Lightman at Cal Tech who have a set of equations that describe all the experimental phenomena that are used to justify the general and special theories of Relativity, but which would permit faster than light travel, that may satisfy all the experimental evidence. Now Lee and Lightman don't claim that they have a better set of equations for the universe than Einstein, and certainly they are less elegant than Einstein's equations, but they do satisfy all known evidence and permit faster than light travel. Now isn't that interesting? And this is a pair of graduate students at Cal Tech who were given the job of taking all the known data on Relativity and coming up with some way of discarding either the Einstein General Theory or Dickey's equations or something, and what they did was they ended up with some of their own which worked just as well, and they couldn't discard anything.

Q. Wouldn't it be desirable in a hard science story to get a more accurate speculation by not violating *any* of the present rules?

Pournelle: It gets hard then to distinguish between science fiction and mainstream novels.

Q. For example, if you were to speculate on a technological or social development which doesn't violate any *known* science—

Pournelle: I've done that in stories with the name Wade Curtiss on them rather than my own, but that's known to be my name now that somebody made the mistake of copyrighting a Wade Curtiss book in the name of Jerry Pournelle. I've done a number of them in which the assumptions didn't violate anything. They take present day technology and project it ten years. That's one way to write a story.

Q. Do you prefer to do it that way?

Pournelle: No, actually I prefer to play games with faster than light travel and things like that. Regeneration.

Q. How far can you get before you lose touch with present knowledge?

Pournelle: I don't know. Larry Niven and I did a story which is set in the year 3000 and it looks pretty good to us.

Q. Hard science type science fiction was certainly the original variety as far as genre science fiction goes. Which of the early writers do you think are the most important and which do you particularly admire?

Pournelle: Well, in my judgment the most important man in science fiction is Robert Heinlein. And the second most important one was John Campbell. And one of the reasons John Campbell was important was because he wouldn't buy a story by Robert Heinlein. Robert wrote a story called "It's Great To Be Back"—or maybe it was "The Green Hills of Earth," one of those stories that Robert wrote during the 1940s—and John didn't like it. Robert sold it to the *Saturday Evening Post* and all of a sudden science fiction went from having a readership of maybe 20,000 which was the circulation of *Astounding* in those days, to eight million which was the circulation of the *Post*. In that time there were maybe two people in the world who made a living at science fiction. Now there are probably twenty-five or thirty who make a living at science fiction, and another four hundred people who can at least claim to be more or less professional science fiction writers. He must have touched a nerve. He did something.

Q. Heinlein did something, but is this to Campbell's credit or just a freak accident?

Pournelle: No idea. The fact remains that when Heinlein's stuff was in the *Saturday Evening Post* the field was able to support a lot more people than it was before, and consequently I suppose that all of us in many respects owe Robert Heinlein our livings. I just make a living, you know. I don't try to teach people. I don't try to change the world. I just make a living.

Q. Aside from what Heinlein did to expand the market, why do you admire him as a writer?

Pournelle: Because he was consistent, because he did the game well. He wouldn't just throw an idea into a story because he needed it for the story, and then not consider the consequences. Let me give you an example. Let us take somebody I can talk about. Larry Niven is a very good friend. We've written several books together. Larry has in one of his sets of stories a fusion drive, the so-called single-ships, which work by hydrogen fusion. Now to actually build that you would have to have something that can contain a fusion explosion in a small space, direct its force in one direction and one only, so it can give you drive, right? Some kind of magic screen. Do you not see that if you have that you have everything Poul Anderson wrote about in a story called "Shield"? You have in fact something that will fundamentally change the way in which people live. Larry never bothered with that. He put them in the ships and they go around with them, but people don't have invisible body shields and you can't protect a city from atom bombs and the rest of it. If you have such a device you could protect cities from atom bombs. What does that do? It changes the hell out of the whole nature of military technology if you can build an invulnerable fortress that you couldn't even destroy with a hydrogen bomb, doesn't it?

Q. It does.

Pournelle: All right. It's not considered in his stories. Now this is not meant as some kind of a slam at Larry Niven. He's a damn good writer, but the fact is that Heinlein would never have done that. If he was required to invent something that would change the whole nature of society he would either write the story in which the whole nature of society was changed, or he would have come up with a different kind of invention that didn't produce that result. You see what I'm trying to get at? He didn't just stick something in because it was convenient to this paragraph.

Q. In the Niven story you mentioned he was talking about a way to drive spaceships. Might not any writer save the social implications for a second story?

Pournelle: But he puts it into a context in which you have a normal social structure. If you've got that kind of technology somebody will have exploited it for something besides spaceships. It's inevitable that they will. If I invent a coat of armor that makes me like Superman, I will do more with it than just build a spaceship. If I don't, the guy who paid me to develop it will. Nobody is so dumb that they don't see the implications of a thing like that, if they have it for real. I'm not trying to knock Larry. This isn't an anti-Niven tirade—Larry's one of the finest writers in the business. I have enormous respect for him and I think he does for me. We work so well together I think because we *do* admire each other so much, but Larry made a mistake in that story, as I have in several of mine. Robert doesn't make that kind of error in his stories generally. When he gives somebody a capability he develops the implications of it. That's the difference between really good hard science stuff and the stuff in which people just invent something ad hoc, stick it in the story and use it for a while. And Larry's not the worst offender. I just picked him because I can comfortably talk about it, because I do admire him so much that I don't feel guilty about criticizing him. There are some people who are forever sticking in an invention in this paragraph, and in the next paragraph they write something totally contradictory.

Q. Some writers write for simply making weird effects, and there is no science in it whatever. Does this even belong in a science fiction magazine?

Pournelle: I don't know where you ought to put it. It is not a writer's decision as to what belongs in a magazine. That's the editor's job, and the editor discovers if he has done well within a few months because he ceases to have any readers if he is not giving them entertainment, right?

They stop buying the damn thing. That's a different job from a writer's job.

Q. Getting back to the question you strayed away from, what writers have influenced you and made you the writer you are?

Pournelle: I don't know what you mean by the writer I am. People like my stuff. I don't think anyone thinks it will change the world, including me. Oh, Heinlein, Poul Anderson, and I guess the guy many people compare me to you may not even be familiar with because he's been dead for so long—H. Beam Piper. Beam was an old friend, and I suppose to some extent I write the kind of stuff that Beam used to write. You know, it's sort of fun; it's got a point of view to it; it's intended to entertain and I don't really care if you don't take it seriously just as Beam didn't. I'd say the people who probably influenced me the most in this are the people whose works I enjoy the most, Anderson, Heinlein, Piper, Hal Clement.

Q. What kind of a background do you have for the kind of writing you do, and do you usually end up doing research for your stories?

Pournelle: Sure. I usually manage to get a research assignment from a major magazine that will pay me a couple thousand dollars for an article on something, and then afterwards I use the research to write science fiction stories with. There's more money in non-fiction than there is in fiction. To give you an example, a thing called "Extreme Prejudice" has a sea-based power plant in it. The power plant concept would work. The engineering is all worked out in the story, and the reason it is all worked out in the story is that *American Legion* gave me about $1500 to do an article on the subject. I did the research for that and when I was finished with it I knocked off a story in which that technology was used. That was free. I think you'll find that most science fiction writers like me don't spend much time reading science fiction. We don't have the time anymore. Not that we don't enjoy it anymore—we just don't have the time. I spend most of my time reading non-fiction, science, the latest textbooks. The half-life of an engineer nowadays is seven years. That means that for a guy who graduates from engineering school seven years after he gets out of it, half of what he was taught is useless.

Q. Is your background in engineering?

Pournelle: Yeah, and my half-life is long gone.

Q. Well, you've survived.

Pournelle: Well, that means I have to scramble like hell to keep up. I spent fifteen years in the space program. I was part of the old Project Mercury. I was in charge of certain aspects of the human factors program, keeping people alive in space. I did a lot of technological forecasting. I used to tease Heinlein and say I wrote more science fiction than he did and got paid more per word, and I didn't have to come up with characters and plots. All I had to do is come up with the settings. That was technological forecasting.

Q. The space program has been under a lot of criticism recently. What's your answer? Why should we continue, and what benefits will come out of it?

Pournelle: Why should a Queen named Isabella have financed a crazy character named Columbus? What benefits could she foresee from it? As a matter of fact it damn near bankrupted Spain before it was all over because it made life so easy for them that they stopped doing anything else, but for Western civilization it was no bad thing. What do you want? Do you want pure economic benefits of the space program? The space program cost maybe twenty billion bucks. I can show you that at least ten billion of that was saved in more accurate weather forecasting. I am just right there, writing it off, the fact that I know a hurricane is coming, evacuate and prepare for it and so forth. I can show you economic benefits in crop forecasting. We used to say that one of the things the Russians were going to do when they were playing the Soyuz game before they knocked off their three guys—and that's an interesting story as to why they did it because the commander kept saying, "Hey, don't bring us down yet," but they did, because they control their ships from the group, while we control ours from inside. The captain's in charge—we used to say that one of the things the Russians were going to do in the Soyuz program was they were going to get up there and get an accurate forecast for the grain crop for the coming year and they were going to make about two hundred million dollars just playing the commodities market. You *could*. Does this sink in what I'm trying to say, that just the more accurate prediction of agricultural yields and so forth? People spend a great deal of money to come up with that. Crop flights. We found a large number of natural resources in Africa that were never before suspected, and we found them because a couple of guys stuck a hand-held camera out the window and shot a couple of pictures and when the pictures were published it turned out that they showed some features that you could only see from orbit, that you couldn't have seen from an airplane.

Q. Will the immediate benefits be focussed on the Earth, or will something of obvious value come from beyond?

Pournelle: Well, nearer space has the greatest and most immediate enonomic benefit. I think that's fairly obvious. That doesn't mean that it isn't worthwhile looking beyond it. Orbital space is a worthwhile proposition for stockholders. You can make a profit out of it. I mean I'd buy stock in a company that's getting involved in it because I would expect to get rich out of it. Lunar and Martian exploration—sure I'd buy a little stock in it, figuring that my great-grandchildren would come up with something. Now is it an obligation of the people of this century to invest money for their great-grandchildren? I'm willing to do it. Are you? I don't know.

—Discon II, 1974

117

Afterword

INTERVIEWING THE INTERVIEWER

Note: The person playing the part of A is highly questionable. The person playing the part of Q is unanswerable.

Q. How did you get started interviewing?

A. The same way they taught kids to swim in simpler times. I was thrown into it without warning or experience and learned awfully quick. I was writing reviews for a Philadelphia paper called *The Drummer* and its companion *The Daily Planet* (No, Clark Kent didn't work there. He was fired before my time for exposing himself in a company phonebooth.) and the idea of doing an interview occurred to me. So I called up the editor and he thought it was a good idea too, and we were all set. But before I got a chance to break the news to the intended interviewee, he had left the country. (A coincidence, you understand.) I tried again and found another local SF pro, Gardner Dozois, who was willing. *The Drummer* was willing also, so I made an appointment with him. I was at this time totally inexperienced in the art of interviewing. Never tried it before.

Q. And what happened?

A. The tape recorder broke. I was also totally inexperienced at the art of running tape recorders. You see, mechanical failure is the interviewers greatest fear. It's rather embarrassing to take up somebody's time like that and then be unable to do the interview, or, worse yet, get home *afterwards* and discover that it didn't record. I test carefully before each interview, and during the interview I periodically check to see if the little spools are still moving. In this first attempt Gardner and several other people tried to get the damn thing operating. Finally we did.

Q. Then what happened?

118

A. The tape proved to be defective. Really. I'm not making this up. The tape wasn't inside the cartridge properly. Now I had another tape with me, but it contained a psychological report. The owner of the machine had left it in. I knew it was old, and he didn't want it, so I decided to erase the tape. You erase a tape by recording over it, right?

Q. Right.

A. Maybe it works that way in the White House, but my tape just wouldn't erase, and the result was a *superimposition*. It sounded like a bad Firesign Theatre routine and went something like this:

> Me: This is Alpha Baker Charlie calling Hot Buttered Cockroach. Testing. Testing.
> A Deep Voice: There are three kinds of love. I will describe them for you. . .
> Somebody in the background: What's that?
> Somebody else: That's Ronnie's sex report.
> Gardner: I hope she did the original research for it.
> Somebody: No, Frank did it all for her.
> Deep Voice: Being Love, Eros. . .
> Gardner: We have here *Chains of The Sea,* three original novellas of science fiction by Gardner R. Dozois, George Alec Effinger and Darrell Schweitzer. . .
> Me: No wonder it only sold three copies.
> Deep Voice: The meaning of Eros is. . .

And so on. I got the interview a few days later, with the help of a technical advisor. Even then we had trouble. Chipmunk sounds and the like. I have the magic touch with tape recorders.

Q. Do you research and prepare your questions before each interview?

A. Research, never. Sometimes I read a critical essay by the person first (see the Bester interview, for example) or listen to a speech by him so I have a few starting points, but prepared questions are much too rigid. I used a set of them for Sprague de Camp and he tended to render questions five through nine redundant while he was still answering question two. I saw that this would never work, so I stopped using prepared questions. I ad lib everything. I have been known to meet someone by chance at a convention and ask him for an interview, without any prior preparation on the part of either of us. I rely on my knowledge of the field, and the interviewees rely on having the sort of brain that produces fascinating books.

Q. Don't you ever get disappointing results?

A. I did once, and that one will probably never be published. I won't say who it was with, but it seems I didn't know enough about the guy ahead of time. In general the only rule of thumb you can follow is this: interview someone whose work you personally respect. It is not a good

119

practice to do somebody whose work you have never read, though I have done it, I interviewed people I never heard of on two occasions, both of them outside of SF. One was a dream psychologist, and the other was a rabbi who believed that the God of the Old Testament was an alien. "If you want to know about space travel, you have to read the Bible in the original tongues," he kept saying. In both cases the opening question was something like "Tell me about your work," and the interviews were quite good, or so *The Drummer* editor thought. Maybe I was just lucky.

Q. Do you ever use stock questions?

A. Yes, occasionally to get an interview started, or to get it moving when it has started to drag. Some of the basics are, "How did you become a writer?" "What attracted you to SF?" and, to wrap up I often ask what books are forthcoming. Sometimes I toss something completely random like, "What do you think are the principle values (faults, strengths) of contemporary SF?" and see what he thinks about that. But of course a good interview can't lean on these too heavily. A question yields an answer which is the genesis of the next question. The interplay is like that of a normal conversation, perhaps a little formal, but nevertheless it is a *conversation*, not an interrogation. That's why I never do interviews through the mail. No good. No flexibility.

Q. What do you mean by a 'good interview?'

A. A good interview is one that I would want to read if somebody else did it. In general I like interviews in which the interviewer plays an absolutely minimal role. The reader is interested in the interviewee and what he has to say, not the interviewer. He's of no importance. He plays a role like the Host in the *Canterbury Tales*. His function is to prod other people into saying interesting things. Look, when I was in college there was a guy who did interviews (if you could call them that) for the campus paper. He somehow got to know famous people, mostly singers, actors, and directors. Famous showbusiness types. He never once published a decent interview because he'd hog all the space for himself, even the photos. It would be a picture of Joe X, all ego and no discernable talent, with someone of note in the background. The interview itself was all about how *he* went to a certain city, how *he* met a famous celebrity, how *he* said this and *he* said that, and the person allegedly being interviewed was just quoted in passing once or twice. Not only was it shockingly bad journalism but it gave me a strong prejudice in favor of the question and answer format, as opposed to the profile and personal impression approach.

Q. Do you edit your interviews much?

A. My own questions, yes. I often phrase them poorly, making them up as I go along, talking in first draft you might say. As Delany says in *Dhalgren* somewhere, editing your own transcripts provides one of the few chances you have to be articulate. Usually the writer being inter-

120

viewed requires little editing. He has usually spoken in public before (I never have) and may have been interviewed before. He's more used to speaking in a clear, concise and organized manner. Besides, he's not on the spot as much, since in most cases the interviewer has to lead the conversation, and the interviewee simply responds to questions. I don't edit the responses unless sentences trail off and end nowhere as the writer changes the focus of his attention, or unless he has a habit of repeating phrases or saying "um" a lot. The answers are printed virtually verbatim. Less chance of misquoting this way. Interviews certainly have gotten more accurate with the invention of the tape recorder.

Q. What good are interviews? Why do people read them and why do magazines publish them?

A. Magazines publish them because people read them, and people read them, I think, because they want to know more about the author. Especially on a paperback book the author is a faceless name, and if you liked the book you often want to know what kind of a guy he is, and so on. Remember what Holden Caulfield said in *Catcher in the Rye*? A good book is one that makes you want to call up the author. Well, you can't call up the author—he hasn't the time and if you tried he'd get his number unlisted—so an interview is the next best thing.

Q. Why do authors give interviews?

A. Hey, I like that. I ought to ask one sometime at the end of an interview. No, I think I can answer that one myself. An author is usually eager to give an interview because of the egoboo of seeing himself written up in some magazine, and more than that there is his desire to promote his own books. There's nothing wrong with self-promotion. In today's world you have to do it. Consider: when Gardner Dozois' interview appeared in *The Drummer* the paper was deluged with calls and letters asking where they could get his stuff. Alas, Gardner didn't have any novels or story collections on the stands at that time, so all that got sold were extra copies of his anthology, *A Day In The Life*. I'm sure it didn't hurt.

Q. Do they ever turn down an interview offer?

A. Isaac Asimov turned me down, but that's because he is, as somebody once put it, one of America's leading natural resources. Everybody knows about him and he doesn't need to give interviews. Also he has been interviewed so many times he's tired of it. He said so in his letter. The magic does wear off after a while, I'm sure. Also, Barry Malzberg refused very graciously when I approached him at Lunacon last year. He said I should read *Herovit's World* and that would tell me everything I wanted to know about him. *Herovit's World* is about a crazy, paranoid science fiction hack writer who is rapidly becoming unglued.

Q. What effects does extensive interviewing have on the interviewer?

121

A. Many. First it gives him the opportunity to meet a lot of interesting and often charming people. Second, it may not make him rich but it does provide a little extra cash. There's nothing wrong with that, of course, since it isn't the *writer* who forks up the dough. Both the writer and the interviewer benefit from a good interview. Third, if the interviewer is a fiction writer himself it helps him write better dialogue. If you have any sensitivity for language at all you can't help but notice individual speech patterns after you've transcribed a couple interviews. Fourth, it makes him a better conversationalist because it teaches him when to shut up and listen. If you keep talking yourself, interrupting your own interview, the train of thought gets broken and the results are lousy. Always let the interviewee go on as long as he wants on a given topic. The most interesting material comes out this way, often volunteered on the side, something you never would have thought to ask. If you mess up the interview you've wasted everybody's time because it'll never be published. Interviewing other people is excellent therapy for compulsive talkers.

Q. Maybe we ought to end this.

A. Yes. After all, nobody bought the book on the strength of the afterword. Let's not overstay our welcome.

Afterthoughts:

We went off on a tangent there, at the end, but I think the points I made remain valid ones. However, some of the points mentioned earlier need updating.

The "potential backer" I spoke of turned out to be egotripping on the idea of becoming a publisher. He was apparently never serious at more than playing with the idea of buying the magazines, and subsequently dropped the notion. He acts embarrassed when he sees me now. So much for plans to change the formats of *Amazing* and *Fantastic*, the five-person well-salaried staff, and new magazines.

My own Doc Phoenix appeared in *Weird Heroes* vol. 2, published December, 1975. I haven't finished the novel yet—and finding myself talking about writing it last June was a jolt—but Pyramid is waiting for it rather impatiently and I'm working on it now. (Writing a book while editing two magazines and taking care of a five-year-old daughter is not nearly as easy as writing books used to be when I was living alone and reading *F&SF's* slush pile.)

I do not expect to be editing *Amazing* and *Fantastic* much longer; I recently finished the 50th Anniversary issue of *Amazing* and found myself writing a rather pessimistic editorial for it. In part this is because the publisher axed the plans I had for celebrating *Amazing's* 50th—nearly every idea I'd developed over the past six years was enthusiastically accepted and then whittled down to nothing. But *Amazing's* sales are disastrously low and I'm not sure whether I'll leave the magazines first or they'll disappear right out from under me. I expect I'll know, one way or the other, by mid-1976.

—Ted White
February, 1976

www.ingramcontent.com/pod-product-compliance
Lightning Source LLC
Chambersburg PA
CBHW020658180626
46816CB00003B/1342